ROMANTIC RESUMES

What Graduate School Did For Lovely Young Jane Doe

Veronica Verity

Edited by John Marriott
Author of *Desperado's Woman* and *The Masks of Imogen*
A Columbine Romance

Order this book online at www.trafford.com
or email orders@trafford.com

Most Trafford titles are also available at major online book retailers.

Printed in the United States of America.

ISBN: 978-1-4269-8881-3 (sc)
ISBN: 978-1-4269-8882-0 (e)

Trafford rev. 06/15/2012

 www.trafford.com

North America & international
toll-free: 1 888 232 4444 (USA & Canada)
phone: 250 383 6864 ♦ fax: 812 355 4082

To the memory of my parents
Eric Leslie Marriott, 1895-1981
and
Eva Florence L'Ami Marriott, 1895-1983

CONTENTS

AUTHOR BIOGRAPHY

Veronica Verity is the *nom de plume* of John Eric Marriott who was born in 1931 in Saskatoon, Saskatchewan—perhaps the only city to have been named for a berry—where he grew up, received his elementary, secondary and undergraduate education. He has been an Anglican parish priest, high school English teacher, an unsuccessful husband, a reasonably successful parent, a university lecturer and something of a perpetual student, having obtained his PhD in English on his second try from the University of British Columbia in 1994 at the age of sixty-three when it was too late to do him or anyone else much good. After being put out to pasture in 1995, he began writing in earnest, initially simply for his own amusement until a friend, no doubt with the best of intentions, urged him to submit himself to the rigors of trying to become published. He has written eleven novels, most unpublished. He lives in Vancouver, British Columbia. As Abraham Lincoln noted in his autobiograhy, "No other marks or scars remembered."

AUTHOR'S NOTE

The characters Jane Doe, Manuel Fernando de Ortega y Diaz de Rodriguez and Yvette La Flambee, as well as suggestions for several of the episodes of this novel, are the brain children of Elizabeth Emond, my editor John Marriott's former fellow graduate student at the University of British Columbia, and that of Percy Byron Browning the creation of Sarika Bose, another of his former fellow graduate students at the same Institution of Higher Learning, both of whom have since earned Doctorates, the former from UBC, the later from Birmingham. John relayed these ideas to me in the anticipation that I might be able to develop them, but all blame for the manner of that development lies with me.

V. V.

ACKNOWLEDGEMENTS

The author gratefully acknowledges the posthumous assistance of Sir Thomas Wyatt the Elder, William Shakespeare, John Milton, Thomas Gray, Robert Burns, Charlotte and Emily Bronte, Artemus Ward, Charles Dickens, Alfred Lord Tennyson, William Ernest Henley, Sir William Schwenk Gilbert, Rudyard Kipling, Stephen Leacock, Cole Porter, P. G. Wodehouse, Sir Winston Leonard Spencer Churchill, Leonard Q. Ross, and Charles Schultz in the writing of this novel.

V. V.

CHAPTER THE FIRST

Her pony tail in which she tied back her long, voluptuous blond locks bobbing up and down with every step she took, lovely young Jane Doe skipped lightly up the steps of the dingy, dimly lit stairwell toward the English Department Reading Room on the sixth floor of the Buchanan Tower—from inside which one was spared the sight of the principal eyesore on the campus of the University of British Columbia.

"Am I just too literary for my own good," she wondered as she ascended, "or is there really something ominous, perhaps even momentous and portentous, in the fact that every time I climb these stairs I always think of Edgar's line in King Lear—which is, of course, also the title of a poem by Robert Browning—'Childe Roland to the Dark Tower came'?"

Jane had come from the free, open, clean and innocent Canadian Prairies—though some, no doubt, would dispute the claim of freedom, cleanliness and innocence of those Prairies, but none would deny their openness—to study for her Ph.D. at the vast, sprawling, intimidating, intellectually over-sophisticated but lushly lovely campus of the University of British Columbia in the immense, far-flung, worldly-wise—and just plain worldly—somewhat decadent, perhaps even slightly wicked, but— Jane had to confess—rather exciting and certainly gorgeously situated and—if only the mountains did not block the view—scenic West Coast Canadian port city of Vancouver.—

As she mounted the stairs, she heard on the stairs below her a footfall—a very masculine footfall.

—I hope to goodness, she thought, even though she knew, as Linus had pointed out, that hoping to goodness was not theologically sound, that is not the very masculine footfall of Manuel Fernando de Ortega y Diaz de Rodriguez!

Manuel Fernando de Ortega y Diaz de Rodriguez was the haughty, arrogant and—again Jane found herself compelled to confess—darkly handsome Spaniard who had also registered this same year as she in the Ph.D. program and, whether by coincidence or by design she was uncertain, had also registered in the same classes as she: Bibliographical Methods and Research—which, Jane had to acknowledge, was compulsory and everyone had to take—Shakespeare and Donne, and in each one of them, it was quite evident that Manuel Fernando of the multiplicity of surnames "had eyes" for her. In fact, he more than just "had eyes" for her. As her friend Catherine, who did not suffer from Jane's cultivated reserve and genteel inhibitions, stated bluntly, "Watch out for that Manuel Fernando de Ortega y Diaz de Rodriguez. He undresses you with his eyes every time he looks at you." Jane, who could not bring herself to such bluntness, felt that he *was,* in fact, looking at her as though she were n—na—as though she were n—nu—as though not w—w—wearing—as though she had left her dress in the closet and her—her—un—un—her unmentionables in the dresser drawer. Now, Jane knew she had much to learn about life and thought that perhaps there was no better place to learn it than here on this vast, sprawling, intimidating, intellectually oversophisticated campus of the University of British Columbia in this immense, far-flung, worldly-wise—and just plain worldly—somewhat decadent, perhaps even slightly wicked, but rather exciting West Coast Canadian port city of Vancouver, but she had not been prepared for the like of the haughty, arrogant but—as noted, she had had to confess—darkly handsome Manuel Fernando de Ortega y Diaz de Rodriguez.

—Why, she wondered, has he come here to Vancouver to study at UBC when he could attend any one of the renowned universities in one or other of the fleshpots of Europe? And why is he interested in a simple, ordinary girl like me from the free, open, clean and innocent Canadian Prairies when back home he could probably have a duchess or a countess? Oh, I suppose I am rather pretty, and perhaps I should be flattered by his attention, but I've heard about these Latin Lotharios, and I do not want to be the side dish to his main course. Especially after my experiences with Donald!

Jane and Donald had dated when they were both in the Master's Program at the University of Saskatchewan in Saskatoon—a lovely charming little Prairie city on the banks of the South Saskatchewan River where Jane had been born and where she had grown up and attended school. (Again, many would say that it had once been charming before its civic leaders became afflicted with a severe case of Biggerandbetteritis in the years following the Second World War.) Her relationship with Donald had progressed from coffee after class to movies on the weekends and the occasional play or concert, and she had begun to think he and she had much in common until one evening Donald had propo—proposi—had made untoward ad—adv—advan—had tried to—to—Jane could not bring herself to name what Donald had tried to—to—

Well, all that was behind her now—or at least so she fervently hoped. Donald had gone East to York University in that *extremely* decadent, wicked city of Toronto—pronounced by the natives "Tirana" like the capital of Albania—which thought itself the centre of the universe and to whose denizens the West is Sarnia—a statement in which some claim to hear an echo of the last words spoken by Shakespeare's Hamlet. To be as far away as possible from Donald was one of Jane's reasons for accepting the offer of a Teaching Assistantship—affectionately known by those so honored as a T.A.—at this vast, sprawling, intimidating, intellectually oversophisticated Campus of the University of British Columbia—affectionately known by its students and alumni as UBC—at the opposite end of the country. Yes, Jane hoped, Donald was out of her life for good, but the memory of him and what he had—had—what he—of what she could not name was enough to make her leery of further romantic entanglements, especially with the like of Manuel Fernando de Ortega y Diaz de Rodri—guez. If ever there was a Don Juan, it was he.

—Although, thought Jane, as her imagination conjured up unbidden the image of his exotically aristocratic good looks and his embarrassingly extravagant politeness, perhaps it's just that I've never met a Spaniard aristocrat before. Perhaps everything that bothers me about him is simply part and parcel of his world, and I just have to get used to it. Oh! What am I thinking!

And now, once again, Jane heard below and behind her that imperious and decidedly masculine tread drawing ever closer as though the treader was following and trying to overtake her. With a shudder, she quickened her own pace and arrived at the Reading Room slightly out of breath.

"Did you run all the way up?" asked Alison Auchinleck, (third cousin five times removed of the British General to whom German Field Marshall Irwin Rommel attributed his defeat at Alamein) who was working her way through the Ph.D. program by serving as Reading Room attendant. Slightly older than most of her fellow students—all except Ron Harriott, probably the oldest Graduate student currently in captivity—she took a kind, motherly interest in their well-being. "It's not good to sit in a sweat, you know."

"Wha—? Oh, no," replied Jane. "It's a long climb, that's all. Good for the cardiovascular system."

"Yes, I suppose you could say that for it," responded Alison. "Anyway, welcome to the Reading Room, Jane. I believe it's your first visit."

"Yes. I want to research the Pollard and Redgrave *Short Title Catalogue*."

"An inestimable scholarly research tool for those interested, as I believe you are, Jane, in the English Renaissance," said the knowledgeable and ever helpful Alison. "It's right back there on the shelf against the north wall."

"Thanks," said Jane, and she made her way to the shelf indicated by Alison. She had just located the volume of the inestimable scholarly tool for students of the English Renaissance—one of which, indeed, she was—when she heard Alison greet another person entering the Reading Room.

Jane felt her whole body shudder as she heard the new arrival greet Alison in Spanish. *"Ah! Buenos dias, Senorita."* So the masculine footfall on the stairs *had indeed* been that of him whom she so greatly dreaded meeting! The speaker could be none other than Manuel Fernando de Ortega y Diaz de Rodriguez!

With a more than scholarly assiduity, Jane scanned the pages of the *Short Title Catalogue of Books Published in England, Scotland, and Ireland and of English Books Published Abroad, 1475-1700* by A. W. Pollard and R. G. Redgrave—fondly known to scholars as the *STC*—but somehow her efforts at concentration made her only more flustered, for as she stared at the page, all she saw were dancing letters—or was she simply thinking of a movement from Schumann's Carnaval?

"So," said Manuel Fernando de Ortega y Diaz de Rodriguez, continuing his chat with Alison Auchinleck, "this is the Reading Room. A most charming corner of this lushly lovely, even though somewhat intimidating and intellectually over-sophisticated, campus."

"I'm very fond of it," said Alison, speaking with proprietary pride. "I do wish more of our fellow students would make use its resources."

"They do not often come here?" asked Manuel Fernando etc., etc. "That is indeed a pity. But I see at least one who does. *Perdona, Senorita.*"

—Oh dear! reflected lovely young Jane Doe from the free, open, clean and innocent Canadian Prairies. There's no one else here but me! Oh horror of horrors! He's coming over here!

Jane buried herself even more deeply in the pages of the *Short Title Catalogue*, trying to absorb the information on the books published in the year fifteen eighty-eight, but her efforts to appear engrossed in arduous and assiduous research did nothing to dissuade the arduous, assiduous and romantic ardor of Manuel Fernando of what seemed to her, even though she recognized that Spanish traditions were undoubtedly different from those of Anglo-Saxon countries, a rather excessive number of surnames who now stood almost palpably close to her and exuding his powerful masculinity.

"Ah! *Senorita* Doe!" he said, clicking his heels and making a formal bow. "I see our interests are in the same work."

"Oh!" said Jane, looking up in rather poorly feigned surprise. "*Senor* Ortega y Diaz de Rodriguez!"

"Oh do please call me Manuel!" he responded feelingly. "And I hope I may call you Jane?"

"Oh—well—everyone else does—and it *is* my name—so I suppose it's all right—if you want to. Ours is a less formal society, I believe, than yours, *Senor* Orte—uh—Manuel."

"I do want very much to be able to address you by your praenomen 'Jane,' Jane" he replied with a polite inclination of his head, "but I confess to some perplexity that one so lovely as you should have such a simple, ordinary name as 'Jane Doe'."

Jane could not help blushing at the compliment that she was lovely, but then her blush turned immediately to an angry red at his calling her name "simple" and "ordinary"—even though it was.

"My name may be simple and ordinary, *Senor*," she responded hotly, mustering all her dignity and drawing herself to her full height, "and I may be but a simple ordinary girl from the free, open, clean and innocent Canadian Prairies, but I am not ashamed of my name. My family has borne it with honor for many generations as pioneers breaking the sod and sowing and reaping the grain to provide sustenance for our people and for people around the world, and as soldiers defending their country in war!"

"Ah! *Perdona, Senorita* Doe!" he responded apologetically. "I meant no offence, and I respect your pride in your name. I did not say there was anything *wrong* with your name. But do you have any other, a—how do you say?—a middle name?"

"Oh—well—if you must know, my second name is Margaret." Almost she had added, "Not that it is any of your business," but her unfailing good manners forbade her such boldness and effrontery.

"Ah!" sighed Manuel Fernando de Ortega y Diaz de Rodriguez. "Margaret! Marguerita! Jane Margaret! Juana Marguerita! A fine romantic name! A name to be whispered in the gardens of the *Sierra de Cordoba*, to be sung beneath the walls of the *Alhambra*, to be cried aloud from the escarpment of the *Estramadura*!"

"Oh—dear me! Misery me, lackaday me! I—I—" stammered Jane in embarrassment—though she had to confess to herself that she was flattered by the effusiveness of his compliments. "I—I really am quite an ordinary girl, and—and I'm quite happy with my ordinary name."

"Ah Jane!" exclaimed Manuel, again with another polite inclination of his head. "You are hardly ordinary, but since it is your wish simply to be Jane Doe, then I shall respect your wish."

"Oh—" exclaimed Jane, rather taken aback by his courteous regard for her wish.

"After all," continued Manuel, "as Shakespeare's Juliet says, 'What's in a name? That which we a call a rose/ By any other name would smell as sweet.'"

"Oh!" exclaimed Jane again in some surprise and not without some feeling of pleasure. "You—you like Shakespeare?"

"I idolize Shakespeare!" he exclaimed. "There is no writer for whom I care more!"

Again Jane was taken by surprise and again she exclaimed "Oh!" for he had expressed her own sentiments, and she found herself having to make the confession, "I—I love Shakespeare too! But—but," she added, "I would have thought that you would have preferred your own writers—Calder—on, Lope de Vega, Cervantes—"

"Ah Jane!" he said, his facial expression registering great pleasure. "You know Spanish literature!"

—Oh dear! thought Jane, deeply disturbed. I wish I had not said that. He'll use it to try to—to—It will encourage him.

Aloud she said, "A—a little—and only in translation. I don't read or speak Spanish."

"Ah, no matter, Jane. We still have much in common."

—Oh dear! exclaimed Jane to herself again. It did encourage him! I wish we did not have anything in common!

"Well—I suppose," she said aloud, "A little—perhaps."

"Very much, I should think," said Manuel Fernando de Ortega y Diaz de Rodriguez, clearly delighted, his dark eyes glowing. "What could bind two people more closely together than a love of the same literature?"

"Oh—I—uh—I mean—that is," stammered Jane, flustered. "I don't mean—I—uh—it's just that—well—"

"Ah, dear lady!" said Manuel consolingly. "Do not be upset, I pray you. I mean no harm. As a stranger in a strange land it is so very rewarding, do you not think, to find one who shares one's interests? Just suppose you were studying at Barcelona or Madrid."

"Oh—uh—yes, I—I guess I see what you mean. Uh—" she began uneasily, trying to move the discussion away from the foregoing rather unsettling topic, "h—how do you like Canada, *Senor* Orte—uh—Manuel?"

"Ah! Such a vast, beautiful, exciting land!"

"And—and what made you decide—if I'm not being impertinent in asking—to come to Vancouver to study at UBC?"

—Why, I wonder, did I ask that? wondered Jane, although in fact, as we have seen, she *had* wondered.

"Not impertinent in the least, my dear Jane," said Manuel, perfectly unperturbed. "Both Quadra and Juan de Fuca were my ancestors on different sides of my family, and I simply thought I'd like to see where they had been."

"Oh my goodness!" cried Jane, impressed in spite of herself. "You come from a very distinguished background! I'm just an ordinary girl from the Prairies—a commoner, a peon, a member of the third estate—by comparison."

"As I said before, my dear Jane," he responded with an ingenuous and ingratiating smile she found hard to resist, "you are anything but ordinary. With such beauty and intelligence, you have no need to feel inferior in any way whatsoever."

And again he bowed, and again Jane blushed.

—Oh heavens! said Jane to herself once again. He lays it on with a trowel! But no, that's a rather crude way of putting it. He's quite aristocratic and rather charm—OH DEAR! WHAT AM I THINKING!

"Ah Jane!" said Manuel Fernando of the multiple cognomen, apparently noticing her discomfort. "I embarrass you. Such has not been my intention. Please forgive me. It is just my Spanish way. What I really hoped was that you would be so good as to explain to me the significance of this *Short Title Catalogue* and the great importance the professor this morning attached to it."

"Oh—well—if—as it seems you are—interested in the literature of the English Renaissance," said the always helpful Jane, glad to have the conversation turn to academic matters, "it is of great importance, one might say it is indispensable."

"Indeed?" he said, his dark, romantic eyebrows rising.

"Oh yes!" said Jane, warming to the subject. "You see, it lists all the books printed in English from the time of Caxton's first printing press in 1475 until the Parliamentary ban on printing in 1640—and not just any book, but every printing and new edition of it."

"I am most impressed!" he exclaimed.

"Indeed, for it is the product of great labor involving a great amount of painstaking research by Pollard and Redgrave."

"Ah! No doubt. But," said Manuel, again with that slight formal nod, "it is your great erudition, Jane, that impresses me."

—He flatters me, thought Jane, again feeling a blush heating her cheeks, but he does seem genuinely interested in scholarly matters. Perhaps I misjudge him. Perhaps it is just that his ways are so different from what I'm used to, Perhaps he—Oh dear! she groaned inwardly. Why do I keep thinking these thoughts?

"Oh—well—I—" stammered Jane aloud, lost for words and feeling quite flattered in spite of herself.

"But why," he asked before Jane could recover from her embarrassment and articulate her thoughts, "is it called a *Short Title Catalogue?*"

"Oh," said Jane, glad to have the conversation turn again to purely academic matters, "simply for convenience. Renaissance titles have a way of being rather long. Shakespeare's Pericles, Prince of Tyre, for example was first published as THE LATE And much admired Play, Called Pericles,

Prince of Tyre. With the true Relation of the whole Historie, aduentures, and fortunes of the said Prince: As Also, the no lesse strange, and worthy accidents, in the Birth and Life, of his Daughter MARIANA. As it hath been diuers and sundry times acted by his Maiesties Seruants, at the Globe on the Banckside. By William Shakespeare. Imprinted at London for Henry Goson, and are to be sold at the signe of the Sunne in Paternoster row, &c. 1609.

And so it is listed simply as Pericles, Prince of Tyre."

"My goodness!" he said, his, smoldering darkly handsome eyes fairly popping from their sockets. "Such very great erudition, Jane! I am most impressed! And thank you for explaining all that to me!"

"I suppose, if one is to be a scholar, one must become thorough in one's knowledge of one's field."

—Oh dear! That sounded stiff, stilted, and pedantic—and pompous!

To Jane's surprise, Manuel's response to her stiff, stilted, pedantic and pompous comment was rather surprising.

"Indeed one must," he said. "I hope I shall become as knowledgeable as you. You are an inspiration and a challenge."

Having said this, Manuel Fernando de Ortega y Diaz de Rodriguez gazed at her, his eyes aglow and seemingly piercing right through her.

—He's looking at me as though—He's undr—He's removing my garm—He's looking right through my—my clothing to my—my—He's seeing me as if I were n—n—n—

"Jane?" he asked after gazing at her for some moments. "Do you always wear your hair tied back like that in—what do you call it?—a donkey tag?"

"A pony tail!" protested Jane. "Yes, I do! Why should I not?"

"Ah indeed! A pony tail, to be sure," responded Manuel urbanely apologetic. "Why, you ask, should you not wear your hair thus? For no reason, my dear Jane, other than that it does not become you. You should allow those lovely golden locks to fall freely to your shoulders in long, voluptuous tresses."

"Oh—well—I—" Again Jane felt the warm sensation of a blush coming to her cheeks and found herself feeling decidedly and embarrassingly flattered. Then suddenly, as heretofore, she repressed such feelings. Drawing herself up straight and speaking with great dignity, she said, "I shall wear my hair as I see fit, Senor Manuel Fernando de Ortega y Diaz de Rodriguez, and I should be very pleased if henceforth you cease and desist from attempting to impose your will upon me."

"Jane, dear lady!" protested Manuel Fernando et cetera, et cetera. "I have no wish to impose my will on yours. Though I say only what I believe to be true, I do but give advice—merely make suggestions. But perhaps it is my manner. We Spaniards are of a fiery, proud disposition—at least, so goes the rumor—and we are—I am apt, no doubt, to be rather too assertive and dogmatic for the more restrained and reticent Canadian temperament—eh? I shall endeavor henceforth to be less forceful, more temperate in my approach, but it will not be easy for me, and so I beg your indulgence, dear lady."

"Oh—I—"

—Does he read my thoughts too? wondered Jane. And I do wish he would not call me "dear lady"!

Aloud she said, "I—uh—I—Perhaps I was too hasty—uh—"

"No need to be apologetic, my dear Jane. I ask only that you think on my suggestion. But," he said, again bowing and clicking his heels, "I have taken up far too much of your valuable time."

"I—I do have some research to do."

"As do we all. The life of a scholar is a never ending round of research and discovery, is it not, and is it not also our great joy that it should be?"

"Oh—uh—yes. Yes indeed!"

"And so," he said, to her great surprise and dismay, taking her hand in his and brushing it gently with a chaste and ceremonious kiss, *"Adios, cara senorita."*

And with another bow and a click of his heels, he turned and left her standing there dumbfounded and holding out before herself her recently kissed hand, but then, recovering her composure and sang froid, she shook the said extremity and said, "Yech!"

Taking her place at one of the tables with her copy of *The Short Title Catalogue of Books Printed in England, Scotland and Ireland and of English Books Printed Abroad, 1475-1640*, Jane tried to pursue her research, but thoughts of her interview with Manuel Fernando de Ortega y Diaz de Rodriguez kept frustrating her efforts.

—Long voluptuous tresses indeed! Who does he think he is to tell me how to wear my hair! And kissing my hand like that! What a dandy! A regular Don Juan! And that trim little moustache—like Zorro's. I wouldn't be surprised to learn that he rides around at night on a black stallion and in mask and cape scratching Zs—or maybe Ms—on walls with his rapier. Hmph!

Then as she thought of this ridiculous and highly romantic notion, Jane again felt an unwanted and unwonted blush warming her cheek and a thrill of excitement tingling in her spine. She tried to make herself concentrate on the Modern Language Association's standard for preparing a manuscript, to which she had endeavored to turn her scholarly attention in the hope that a change of subject might relieve her mind of unwanted— and unwonted—thoughts, but somehow even this inspiring subject failed to exercise the same appeal as the exotic Spaniard who seemed so greatly interested in her and whom she found fascinating in spite of herself.

—There is, she reflected, more style and finesse—a kind of Continental charm—I suppose, for I've never been to the Continent—Europe, that is—in bowing to a lady and kissing her hand than in the long, low, lewd whistles and shouts of "Wow! Get a load of those hoo—hoot—" those—those—what I have up front—so typical of North American males.

Again she tried to dismiss such thoughts and return to scholarly concentration.

—I wonder, she asked herself after several minutes of futile endeavor, if I would look more attractive if I were to let my golden locks fall to my shoulders in long voluptuous tresses?

CHAPTER THE SECOND

Sitting at a carrel in the Reading Room a few days after her earlier encounter there with Manuel Fernando de Ortega y Diaz de Rodriguez—her golden locks falling to her shoulders in long, voluptuous tresses (on a trial basis and by her own choice *completely* uninfluenced by anything said to her by the multisurnamed Manuel)—lovely young Jane Doe did not look up from her copy of the Norton Facsimile Edition of *The First Folio of Mr. William/ Shakespeare's/ Comedies,/ Histories & Tragedies./ Published according to the True Originall Copies/ LONDON/ Printed by Ifaac Iaggard, and Ed Blount. 1623.* as the said multi-surnamed Manuel entered, yet she was very much aware of the change wrought in the whole atmosphere of the room by his commanding, arrogant and aristocratic presence. He did not speak to her but walked with measured tread to the stacks, drew down a copy of Sir Walter Gregg's *Bibliography of the English Drama to the Restoration* and went straightway—with the same measured tread—to the third carrel behind hers.

—Why didn't he speak to me? wondered Jane.

She endeavored to focus her thoughts on the textual problems of the opening scene of *Coriolanus*.

—Why should I care whether he speaks to me or not!

After some minutes perusing Gregg's *Bibliography* Manuel Fernando with all those surnames rose from his carrel, walked again with measured tread to the stacks, restored the volume to its correct place—obviously he understood the Library of Congress cataloging system—and took down Alfred Harbage's *Annals of the English Drama, 975-1700, Second Edition* (revised by S. Schoenbaum), Philadelphia, The University of Philadelphia Press, 1964, and returned with it to his carrel.

—Darn him! thought Jane. I was going to use that work next! Why does he always have to use the same works I need and at the same time!

Then, somewhat rueful and shamefast, Jane reflected that twice is not always and that she could just as easily use the first volume of *The Elizabethan Stage* by E. K. Chambers.

About twenty minutes later, Jane closed her copy of the *Norton First Folio Facsimile*, rose from her carrel, walked quietly and sedately to the shelves and correctly replaced it.

—There, Manuel Fernando de Ortega y Diaz de Rodriguez! You are not the only one who understands the Library of Congress system!

Taking down the first volume of Chambers's invaluable study, she made to return to her carrel and became immediately aware of Manuel's fiery, intense, penetrating, but darkly and enigmaticly handsome Spanish eyes perusing her critically.

—He's—he's undr—He's looking at me in that way again!

Eyes narrowed, she returned his gaze with what she hoped was a scornful look which, to her surprise and chagrin, did nothing to avert his stare. She wanted to say, "Keep your eyes to yourself, you lecherous Latin Lothario, and mind your own business and stop undr—stop looking at me as though I were n—na—stop looking at me the way you look at me!" but decided simply to ignore his presence. Again, however, she found that her usually effective silent treatment had no effect whatever on Manuel Fernando de Ortega y Diaz de Rodriguez—nor could she ignore his presence.

"Ah! *Senorita* Doe—Jane," said the lecherous Latin Lothario, rising from his carrel and coming to meet her. "I see you have followed my advice and allowed your golden locks to fall to your shoulders in long, voluptuous tresses."

"I've allowed my golden locks to fall to my shoulders in long, voluptuous tresses, *Senor* Ortega y Diaz de Rodriguez, because *I* want my golden locks to fall to my shoulders in long voluptuous tresses," retorted Jane haughtily, "not because you advised me to do so!"

"Ah! As you will, dear Jane," quoth he, perusing her both admiringly and critically. "But for whatever reason, though those golden cascades are very becoming to you, something is not quite right. The effect is not complete. It is not so stunning as it should be. I remain puzzled, uncertain as to the cause of this effect—or rather, this defect, for this effect defective must have a cause as Polonius said—is it not so?"

"I—I suppose it is," stammered Jane, strangely and inexplicably disappointed that her changed appearance had not created the anticipated impression—though, of course, she had not, let it be said emphatically, made the change to impress Manuel Fernando de Ortega y Diaz de Rodriguez! No. Assuredly not. No.

"*C'est la vie, je pense,*" she said, trying to sound nonchalant.

"*Eh bien! Vous parlez francais,* Jane! *C'est tres bon, cela!*"

"*Mais oui! Nous demeurons ici, au Canada, dans un pays bilingue, vous savez.*"

"*Ah, mais oui! Vraiment! Et c'est commendable que vous avez la parole facile de l'une et d'autre.*"

Unused to compliments, whether in French or English, Jane again felt the flush of a blush warm her cheeks.

"Oh—uh—*Merci, M'sieur,*" she said. "It is the least one can do, after all. *Mais j'ai des études.*"

"*Ah, mais oui, M'am'selle. A bientot.*"

Jane returned to her carrel, sat down and, giving an inner "Hmph!" opened Chambers's volume at the first chapter and began to read.

—Why, she soon found herself wondering, did I ever think of trying to please that arrogant Don Juan! Well, I wasn't trying to please him, actually. I just let my hair down to see how I look with it like that and whether I would like it. Just because he happened to suggest it doesn't mean I did it to please him. I did it to please myself. So there.

She read a little further in *The Elizabethan Stage*.

—Actually, I think I do look very attractive with my hair down. So why is he finding fault?

She read a few more pages.

—Why should I care what he thinks? He is nothing to me. Nothing whatever.

She struggled her way through to the middle of the first chapter.

—I'll just put him right out of my mind.

She read until she had covered three quarters of the chapter.

—Completely.

With great determination she applied herself to *The Elizabethan Stage*, making accurate and detailed notes on 3" by 5"—or 7.6 x 12.7 cm.—filing cards and did not notice the dark clouds building up over the Georgia Strait, clouds which were to give Jane her first experience of a Vancouver rain. But, assiduously and doggedly pursuing her research, she was completely unaware that on the Reading Room windows the first light, almost imperceptible drops of rain which would eventually change the beautiful sunny day on which she had left home in the morning into a wet, miserable one by late afternoon.

At three o'clock Jane rose from her carrel so that she might keep an appointment with her friends April, May, June, Julia, Augusta and Catherine. As she returned *The Elizabethan Stage* to its place on the shelves, she felt the gaze of the fiery eyes of Manuel Fernando de Ortega y Diaz de Rodriguez burning into her back as though, like Superman, he had X-ray vision.

—There he goes again, she thought, trying to undr—looking at me as though I were n—na—removing my cl—cl—cl—

Suddenly, almost on the instant, Manuel Fernando of the multiple surname stood beside her.

"Ah Jane!" he said. "If you will permit me once more to make a suggestion—no more than a suggestion, dear Jane, I assure you—I think I have solved the problem."

"The problem? What problem? I'm unaware of any problem, *Senor* Ortega y Diaz de Rodriguez!" she responded haughtily. (Two can play that game, she thought.)

"The problem of why letting your golden locks fall to your shoulders in long, voluptuous tresses has not had its full effect."

"Oh!" exclaimed Jane blushing. "That problem. I assure you, sir," she continued, pretending she was not in the slightest degree affected by his interest, "that to me it is no problem."

"Ah yes! I perhaps interfere too much."

"Oh—" said Jane, somewhat taken aback by his apparent willingness not to force on her his "solution" to her "problem," for, in spite of herself, she found herself quite intrigued by his ideas on her appearance. "I suppose, sir," she said, trying *not* to show herself intrigued, "if you wish to offer advice—make suggestions—even though they are of no consequence to me—I ought at least to have the good grace to hear them. I am at your disposal, *Senor*."

"Yes, and please, dear Jane, as I said the other day, please call me Manuel."

"Oh—uh—yes—Manuel. Well, I am prepared to listen to what you have to say—Manuel."

"Yes. You see, for your long golden locks to have their proper effect, more height is required—if I may be forgiven my use of the passive voice."

"More height, Manuel? I think I have grown to my full height," said Jane with an unwonted sarcasm which astonished her as she pulled herself up as straight as she could.

Jane was, in fact, a trifle self-conscious that she was a *little* taller than the average for a woman—though not too much so. No giant, but certainly not petite. Everything, though, was in its right place; that is, she was properly and most becomingly proportioned—or so, at least, she had been told.

"Ah yes," said Manuel. "But, Jane, do you never wear heels higher than those 2.54 centimetre* illusion heels?"

A light dawned in Jane's memory, namely that she did not wear high heels because they made her taller than Donald who was of short stature.

But what did Donald mean to her now? But what, for that matter, did Manuel mean to her? What indeed!

"I am quite tall enough as I am, sir—Manuel," she said, with dignity and an ever so slight note of hauteur, her nose rising ever so slightly into the air.

"Ah Jane! Your height is perfect!"

Suddenly Jane realized that Manuel was as tall as his name was long—at least six feet—or 183 centimetres—and that despite her own height she felt somewhat dwarfed beside him—not, of course, that it mattered.

"Furthermore, if I may so," continued Manuel, "everything is in absolutely perfect proportion."

"Oh!" Once again Jane felt a blush warming her cheeks as Manuel concurred with the general opinion.

---

*   One inch, Canada having adopted the metric system. (Ed.)

"Perhaps," Manuel continued further, "you feel you must try to appear petite, or men will ignore you, but the true secret of beauty is be proud of what you are and to show it to best advantage. Stand tall, walk tall, hold your head on high—that is the secret, Jane."

"Oh?" said Jane, intrigued in spite of herself.

"Ah yes! And in 10.16 centimetre heels you would look positively statuesque."

"Ten point one six centimetres—four inches?" Then as an image flitted across her inner eye, she exploded in shock, "Four inches! I'd look like a pros—like a hoo—like a lady of the n—n—ni—like one of those women!"

"Ah no, no, no, Jane! It is true that such women as those to whom you allude cheapen the fashions, but that is not the fault of the fashions. You, Jane, would never look like one of those women! You have too much class, too much elegance, too much refinement, too much grace ever to look like such a person. No, no, Jane! Ten point one six centimetre heels would only enhance your appearance making you look stately, regal!"

"Oh—do you think so?"

"Oh indeed yes!"

"W—well, I—I'll th—think about it," she said as the thought of looking regal registered itself in her mind's eye. "But—but right now, I have an appointment to meet April, May, June, Julia, Augusta and Catherine for coffee."

"Ah! Charming, pleasant and attractive young women indeed, but they pale in comparison to you, Jane."

"Oh now, Manuel!" said Jane, coming to her friends' defence, but nevertheless feeling a bit flattered to hear that she was more attractive than her attractive friends. "Those are my friends of whom you speak! I do not like to hear them disparaged!"

"I mean no disparagement of such worthy young ladies, Jane, and I am happy you have made such friends; but I speak only the truth, for you are indeed the most beautiful woman in the English Department and, from what I have been able to observe in my peregrinations about this vast, intimidating, intellectually over-sophisticated but lushly lovely campus, you are the most beautiful woman in the whole of the University of British Columbia!"

"Oh! Oh! Well, I—uh—you—" Jane stammered, feeling herself turning deeper and deeper shades of red and her cheeks fairly burning. "I—I must go. I—I'm late," she said, hurriedly to hide her embarrassment. "I—I don't want to keep April, May, June, Julia, Augusta and Catherine waiting any longer."

"Indeed not, Jane. I apologize for detaining you and will do so no longer. *Hasta la vista!*"

Again he bowed, clicked his heels, seized Jane's hand and brushed it ever so delicately with his lips.

"Oh—uh—yes—*au rev*—farewell, Manuel Fernando de Ortega y Diaz de Rodriguez," said Jane and hurriedly turned on her one inch or 2.5 centimetre, illusion heels and quickly departed the Reading Room.

—There he goes again, reflected Jane as she crossed the hall to the stairwell, kissing my hand and trying to make me over with his ideas on fashion! I'll not let him do it!

Then she began her descent to the fifth floor of the Buchanan Tower.

—Would I really enhance my appearance and look stately and regal in four-inch heels?

Resolutely as she descended to the fourth floor, she thought, What am I thinking! Why should I care for his fashion ideas! I definitely will *not* buy ten point one-six centimetre heels just because he thinks I'd look well in ten point one-six centimetre heels! Letting my golden locks fall to my shoulders in long, voluptuous tresses is the last change I'll make at his suggestion—not that I did so because of him—that is, because he suggested it!

She continued her descent to the third floor.

—Still, I wonder—I've never worn four inch heels. Perhaps I would look—Ah! No! No!

On the third floor, she turned aside to enter the English Department Office to see if her box contained any mail and found an assortment of notices about forthcoming special lectures, administrative directions concerning her first year English class, notices of student activities and of meetings of the T. A. Union and invitations to parties, all of which dispelled from the forefront of her mind all thoughts of four-inch—or ten point one-six centimetre—heels. Then, after greeting in her wonted friendly manner the secretaries, some fellow students and a professor or two, she left with a high heart—but low heels—and a quiet mind to join April, May, June, Julia, Augusta and Catherine in the Student Union Building—endearingly known as the SUB—for coffee.

*   *   *   *

Later, the rain which had been only a drizzle when she had crossed from the Buchanan tower to the SUB had turned into a downpour as she left that building to catch her bus home, and being from the free, open, clean and innocent Canadian Prairies where it never rains—well, hardly ever—Jane had not thought to purchase and umbrella, and so now she was making her way across Wesbrook Mall to the drugstore in the Village just outside the campus to purchase one, trying, in the mean time, to protect herself as best she could by holding over her head a copy of the award-winning student newspaper *The Ubyssey*, but alas! that journal had not won its awards for keeping off the rain, and she felt she would drown before she could ever obtain an umbrella, for she was already soaked to the sk—to the fl—to her natural condition under her clothes. But just at that moment of intense despair, a flashy red automobile drew up beside her, the passenger door opened and a voice cried out to her. "Jane! Get in before you drown! I'll drive you wherever you want to go."

There was no time to ask questions, and so, crying "Thank you very much!" Jane accepted the offer and hopped into the car to discover that its driver was none other than Manuel Fernando de Ortega y Diaz de Rodriguez—as any reader familiar with this kind of romantic fiction has probably guessed. Therefore she exclaimed, "Manuel Fernando de Ortega y Diaz de Rodriguez! You!"

"I hope," said Manuel as they drove away, seemingly somewhat crestfallen by Jane's reaction, "that you were not expecting someone else, and that I have, thus, prevented your rendezvous. I meant only to assist in the inclement circumstances."

"Oh—no—no," said Jane apologetically, "nothing like that. I wasn't expecting anyone. I—I was surprised, that's all. And thank you, Manuel. This is very kind of you. I do appreciate your stopping for me. I was almost drowned."

"That, indeed, was my impression. You must," he said adopting an admonitory tone, "purchase an umbrella."

"That," said Jane defensively, "was what I was on my way to do when you came by."

"Is that not rather like securing the barn door after the cow has flown the coop?"

"I think you mean," said Jane, suppressing a laugh, "'Like locking the stable door after the horse has been stolen.' And yes," she continued ruefully, "I'm afraid it is." Then returning to her more natural manner of speaking, she continued, "It certainly is raining hard. I've never known rain like this. We do have occasional thunder storms on the Prairies, but I've never known such a constant, continuous downpour such as this. I guess that is why I didn't think to buy an umbrella before coming here."

"Fortunately I was warned by someone shortly after I arrived. Otherwise, I might have been as unprepared as you. My home is in a mountainous region, and the precipitation on the Iberian Peninsula confines itself principally to the open tablelands."

"Oh," asked Jane, thinking of some of the pretentious diction and convoluted sentences she had to correct in her first year English students' essays, "I see, but could you not have said it more simply?"

"Yes, but I'm not sure it's in the public domain."

"Oh yes!" exclaimed Jane, shocked at her own forgetfulness in such an important matter. "I didn't think of that. We must consider Veronica's circumstances. We certainly would not want to be the cause of her being sued for copyright violation."

"Indeed not. John might have noticed it, but we must never presume."

"No," said Jane, "but getting back to the weather, I am told that tornadoes seldom occur here."

"Rather as in Hertford, Hereford and Hampshire in Blighty?"

"I've never visited those counties. But," said Jane, changing the subject and showing great consideration, "I hope I'm not taking you out of your way, Manuel. I was intending to go downtown."

"No, not at all. I'm on my way there myself."

As they passed from the University Endowment Lands—the UEL, initials which had puzzled Jane on her arrival, wondering what the United Empire Loyalists had to do with the University of British Columbia—into the City of Vancouver and traveled along Tenth Avenue toward Alma Street, the warm air from the heater was having its comforting, drying effect, and Jane was already feeling less soaked than when Manuel had stopped for her.

"This is a very nice car," she said. "What make is it?"

"A Lamborghini—an Italian car."

"It—it's very—flashy!" said Jane—the car of a playboy, she thought, the car of a modern-day Don Juan—just the sort of car he would drive.

"I suppose it is, yes," said Manuel in response to her vocal comment. "And I suppose you think it appropriate to a haughty, arrogant Spaniard like me. And yes, I suppose I do seem to play the part of a rake, but really, Jane, our reputation as Don Juans is greatly exaggerated—as Mark Twain said of the reports of his death. We are really a formal, reserved, dignified nation."

—Good heavens! Can he really read my mind! exclaimed a rather surprised and shocked Jane to herself.

"Oh—I—uh—I—uh—no, no—" she stammered aloud. "I thought nothing of the—I mean—it's just that I've never ridden in such a splendid, luxurious vehicle."

"I suppose it is a rather expensive and deluxe means of transporting myself from point A to point B," said Manuel, concentrating, to Jane's great gratification, on his driving. "No doubt I've been spoiled by my upbringing. It would be hard for me to drive anything less—a Ferrari, perhaps, but never a Toyota Tercel. 'What is bred in the bone will out in the bone will out in the flesh,' as your Canadian writer Davidson Roberts says," said Manuel as they turned from Tenth Avenue onto Alma and then onto Broadway.

"Excuse me, Manuel," said Jane, a slight note of triumph in her voice, despite her sincere effort to be polite and not sound superior, "but you mean Robertson Davies."

"Ah yes! Robertson Davies to be sure. How gauche of me."

"Then you have read some of Davies novels?" queried Jane, her admiration rising at this unexpected familiarity with the literature of her home and native land which commanded true patriot love in all its sons and daughters.

"Almost all of them, Jane," he said, as they stopped for a red light. "He has, as I'm sure you are aware, an international reputation."

"Yes, and we are very proud of him."

"As well you should be," he said as the light turned green and they drove on.

"As I said, though I don't read Spanish, I have read Cervantes and some of Lope de Vega and Calderon and Garcia Lorca in translation," said Jane, wanting, though she knew not why, to reaffirm that her interests, too, ranged beyond the narrowly parochial.

"Ah! Now it is my turn to make corrections. It is not 'Sirvantees' but 'Kherbanteethe'," he said, aspirating his k and lithping his eth, "and it is Garthia Lor-r-rccha," he added, tr-r-rilling his r and again aspirating his k sound. "Spanish is a rich, salty, tangy language, and it does have a noble literature, but, I must confess, not the rich treasure house that is your English literature."

"Oh—well—but still," Jane protested, though why so emphatically again puzzled her, "it is a great literature."

"*Gracias*—uh—I mean 'thank you' for the compliment. But—to change the subject rather abruptly—may I ask, Jane, in what month you were born?"

"Oh—June," said Jane at this surprising change of topic. "Why do you ask?"

"Oh, just curious. Early June or late?"

"Early, but what diff—"

"Just as I expected! You are a Gemini!"

"Oh," she said disdainfully. "I suppose I am, but I never put much stock in that sort of thing."

"Ah, but you should, Jane!" said Manuel Fernando de Ortega y Diaz de Rodriguez with great emphasis as they turned off Braodway onto Granville Street to cross the bridge over False Creek to get down town.

"We Spaniards still have a sense of the interpenetration of the material by the spiritual, and of the mystical and mysterious, of the unexplained and the inexplicable in human life. As Hamlet says, 'There are more things in heaven and earth, Horatio,/ Than are dreamt of in your philosophy.' And perhaps in this materialistic North American society and culture—if I may be permitted to say so—a culture given too much to the reasonable and sensible and the practical—good things, of course—but you are a society lacking in imagination. So yes, to some extent I do believe such things as astrology."

"Oh—but what has that to do with me?" asked Jane, feeling there was some truth in Manuel's disquisition on matters Canadian. "And how is it that you knew I was a Gemini?"

"Ah Jane! You are so—how shall I say?—so reticent, so reserved, so constrained, so unwilling to let yourself go, too Canadian, too afraid, perhaps, of your feelings—but I sense another woman inside, a more sensual, passionate woman wanting to get out! You are indeed a double personality, one part of whom suppresses the other."

"Oh my! Oh dear! Good heavens! Dear me! Heavens to Betsy! Misery me, lackaday me! I'm not sure I like the sound of that! And how is it you know all this? What makes you so sure about who and what I really am?"

"As I said Jane, I am Spanish, from an Old World culture that has not yet lost the sense of the mystic."

"But—but—you say we North Americans lack imagination, but surely what you say about me and about astrology is pure fantasy without foundation—what my grandmother would call malarky."

"And perhaps it is, dear Jane, perhaps it is. Yet we cannot dismiss the irrational and the supernatural from our lives."

"Well, no, but—but—"

"Think, Jane, think. Is there not truth in what I say, no matter how I've come to know it? Are you not two people, one on the surface, and another deep within struggling to come out?"

"Oh, I suppose we all have sides of ourselves we don't disclose, that we keep hidden," said Jane, feeling a bit uneasy as the Lamborghini made its way slowly through the downtown traffic past some of the more sleazy establishments at the south end of Granville Street.

"Ah, but it's more than that, Jane! I can see it in your attitude toward me. I both frighten you—and I suppose I can be a bit frighteneing—and at the same time, I fascinate you."

"Oh! Oh!" exclaimed Jane. "Now that," she added, drawing into herself, "is getting personal!"

"Ah, forgive me, Jane! No doubt it is. I'm afraid when I think something I just out with it."

"So I have noticed," said Jane, frigidly.

"And it upsets you. I must learn to be more discrete."

For some moments, stalled at a traffic light, they remained silent, for what Manuel had said, Jane had to confess to herself, had cut close to the bone. However, ever polite as she was she broke the silence to say, "It—it's very kind of you, Manuel, to drive me all this way. I really do hope I've not taken you out of your way."

"My dear Jane! The car, does not get tired. However, though I would have been happy to drive you to Whistler and to the summit of Grouse Mountain, I do have business down town." Then Manuel asked as the light turned green so that they could move again "Where do you wish to go, Jane?"

"Oh—yes—Actually," she exclaimed, suddenly realizing—or thinking she did—where they were, "right here!"

With the rain pelting down to cloud the windshield and her mind in something of a turmoil, Jane mistook the corner of Granville and Robson for the corner of Granville and Georgia and, after quickly thanking Manuel for the ride and jumping out of the Lamborghini, found herself, instead of at the Hudson's Bay Store, in front of La Danieta Shoe Salon. Annoyed, but wishing to avoid being further drenched by the unremitting rain, she took shelter in the entrance way, and found quite fascinating, in spite of herself, the display of shoes in various heel heights in the window. Almost without thinking, as though drawn by some mysterious and irresistible force of fate, she entered the store and found herself before a display of high heeled shoes in various bright colors.

"Ah!" said the proprietor advancing toward her. "*Signorina* is interested perhaps in a pair of shoes? Would she perhaps like to try some on?"

"Oh—I—I—uh—I just—Are these four inch heels?"

—Now why, she wondered, did I ask that?

"*Si, Signorina*, and if I may say so," he said unctuously, "*Signorina* would look extremely fetching—might I say, stately, regal and statuesque in a pair."

"Oh! I—I would?"

Where had she heard those words before?

"*Ah, si*! Very fetching, very statuesque, very regal! Does *Signorina* perhaps fancy a particular color?"

Again, the proprietor's words sounded very familiar.

"They—they are all very—bright."

"*Ah si! Si!* The colored shoes add a certain flair to the Signorina's ensemble. Does the *Signorina*," he asked, eying Jane's dress, "frequently wear blue?"

"Y—yes—and sometimes green."

—And why did I tell him that?

"Ah indeed!" continued the proprietor. "Then may I suggest the *Signorina*'s ensemble would be richly complemented by a pair of red shoes?

Perhaps for more formal occasions, gold or silver, but for more ordinary, less formal occasions, red is most becoming."

"R—r—r—red!"

"*Ah si*, red. Most certainly red. But perhaps, as I suggested, *Signorina* would like to try on a pair so that she may see for herself?"

A glance out the window showed Jane that, though the rain was beginning to let up, it still came down quite hard.

"W—well," she said, "I—I guess that would be all right—but I make no promises to buy, mind you."

"Of course, Signorina, but I think *Signorina* will be delighted with what she sees."

And unfortunately for her will power and her budget, Jane *was* delighted and was even further convinced that a red handbag was necessary to complement the shoes. And so it was, as the rain tapered off to a drizzle, Jane left the shoe salon the owner of a pair of red four-inch heels and a matching red leather purse and her clothing allowance for the next month and a half annihilated. (Fortunately, however, a few days later a letter arrived from her parents containing a cheque for a generous amount, although, because of the efficiency and public dedication of the Canadian Union of Postal Workers, who had first read the return address on the back of the envelope as though it were the on the front and, despite the absence of a stamp, delivered it to her parents and then, when that error was pointed out to them, directed it to Vancouver, Washington, whence, because it would have crossed an international boundary, it was again returned to her parents marked "Insufficient Postage," the letter was not delivered to Jane until two and a half weeks after it had first been mailed. All that confusion with its ultimate resolution and happy outcome, caused Jane to reflect later that her uncertainties over her relationship with Manuel Fernando de Ortega y Diaz de Rodriguez were perhaps just a passing phase, and to realize that matters, as well as the foregoing long, involved complicated sentence—not to mention this one—eventually resolved themselves for the best for heroines of romantic novels.)

*   *   *   *

After Jane had arrived home that evening from her fateful trip downtown and after her supper and the washing up of her dishes and before she studied, Jane hand-washed the lingerie that had been accumulating, because of the pressure of her many assignments, in her laundry hamper and hung them on the make-shift clothes line in her bathroom. Much later, her reading completed and her assignments and teaching notes all prepared for the morrow, she leaned back, stretched, yawned, said, "Time for bed," rose from her desk and walked from the corner of her basement suite that she had designated her study to the one she had designated her boudoir.

On the bed lay where she had drfopped them when she came in the parcels containing her new shoes and purse, and on impulse, she drew out the box and opened it to look at the shoes.

—I never thought I'd ever buy a pair of red shoes, but I must say that when I tried them on at the store, I did rather like them. Let's see them on again.

And so saying, she slipped off her slippers—which is what slippers are meant to do—donned her new footwear and stretched out her legs in front of her to look at the effect.

—Yes, I must say, they are rather fetching—quite striking, eye-catching—and attractive. Manuel said I would look stately and regal in four inch heels. I wonder—do I?

To see whether or not that was the effect, she walked to the bathroom and looked at her reflection in the full length mirror on the back of the door. The effect was indeed quite startling.

—I—I do look quite—fetching—statuesque! But—but when will I ever wear them? They're not really for everyday wear, and I certainly do not intend to wear them to impress Manuel Fernando de Ortega y Diaz de Rodriguez! He'll think I bought them because he advised me to, and I most certainly did not!

—At least, she thought, as she left the bathroom to return to her sleeping area, I don't think I did. He didn't tell me to get red ones, after all. But I'm really not sure why I bought them, she thought as she began to undress.

—Oh! A nighty! Do I have one that's dry?

Still wearing her new shoes, she stepped over to her dresser and opened a drawer.

—Oh good heavens! I don't have one—except—Oh good grief!—this!

From the drawer she withdrew and held up before herself by its thin spaghetti straps a very brief, very sheer negligee which she had never worn because Donald had given it to her as a birthday present shortly before he had tried to s—se—sed—before he had tried to f—f—f—tried to de—depr—deprive her of her—to do what he had tried to do that was just too horrible to think of.

"Oh dear! Oh mercy me!" she exclaimed aloud. "Have I nothing else? Oh me, oh my! It—it's utterly transparent. If anyone were to see me in it he—or she, I suppose, but a "he" is what this sort of garment is really designed for—could see right through to my sk—my fl—He could see my wh—whole b—bo—bod—everything that there is to see of me! Why on earth did I ever bring it?"

And then she thought of Manuel's comment that there was a sensual, passionate woman locked inside her struggling to get out.

—Oh goodness! Is Manuel right? Was it that woman—if she really is inside me trying to get out—who made me subconsciously decide to bring it? Oh dear! Oh misery me! Lackaday me!

She stood silently dumbfounded for some moments.

—Well, I—I suppose, she thought at last, there's nothing to do but to wear it. I've nothing else, and no one is going to see me.

She removed her slip and her b—br—her unmentionables and pulled on the negligee over her head, sat on the bed to remove her shoes and peel off her hose, but then, on a sudden and inexplicable impulse, rose again and walked to the bathroom to see in the mirror the effect of the transparent negligee with her red four-inch heels.

—Oh goodness me! I look very s—se—sed—seduc—I look—s—se—I look rather nice.

Again on an impulse, she performed a little pirouette before the mirror and contemplated her reflection again.

—I do have rather nice legs and these four inch heels do show them off rather well. I do look quite splendid in them. And Manuel was right on another count. All the rest of me is in the right places and well proportioned. I have a rather fine b—bo—bod—to—tor—tors—figure, and my b—br—brea—my bo—bos—these things, she said, touching them, are rather nice too. Oh dear! Why am I thinking these thoughts! I bought these shoes to please myself, not Manuel—didn't I? Oh dear, oh dear! Well, I'm certainly glad Donald never saw me in this negligee—and I'm even more certainly glad Manuel Fernando de Ortega y Diaz de Rodriguez can't see me like this!

She turned out the light and left the bathroom to return to her bed.

—Or am I? Oh! Oh! Oh dear! What am I thinking!

She seated herself on the bed and removed her shoes and her hose.

—Yes, of course I'm glad he can't see me.

She placed her shoes by the side of the bed.

—Definitely.

She got into bed and pulled up the covers.

—Those shoes are really very nice, she thought. Perhaps tomorrow, just for that one time, I will wear them—but for myself, not for Manuel Fernando de Ortega y Diaz de Rodriguez.

She sighed.

—This negligee is not very warm, she reflected as she snuggled down. But then, it's not really meant for warmth. It's meant for—for—what I certainly would not want Manuel Fernando de Ortega y Diaz de Rodriguez to see me in it for.

She pulled up the covers as high as they would come.

—Good heavens! I'd fail a student for writing a sentence like the one I just said—thought—formulated.

A yawn escaped her as she snuggled down as deeply as she could into the bed clothes.

—I'm tired. It has been quite a day.

Again she yawned.

—Yes, quite—a—day . . .

And she drifted off into sleep.

*　　*　　*　　*

At a dance in the SUB ball room, her golden locks falling to her shoulders in long, voluptuous tresses and wearing her red shoes, but instead of an evening gown, her sheer negligee, Jane waited for someone to ask her to dance and wondered why no one had done so, when suddenly a leering viciously wolfish-looking creature who resembled Donald advanced menacingly toward her.

"So," he drooled, "you've finally dressed like the sexy doll I want you to be!"

"I'm dressed, sir," said Jane with dignity, "to please myself, and no one else. I dress this way because I want to dress to dress this way."

"That's okay by me, Babe," said the leering, viciously wolfish looking creature who resembled Donald, "because that's the way I want you to dress—with nothing left to the imagination." Then grabbing her by the arm, he said, "Come on, Babe. We're gonna dance."

"Release my arm, sir!" protested Jane. "I do not wish to dance with you!"

"You're gonna dance with me," he snarled, dragging her onto the dance floor, "whether you want to or not, and after that—"

"No!" cried Jane! "Oh! Somebody! *Au secours*! Help! Save me! *Sauvez moi*!"

"Nobody ain't gonna save, ya, Babe, 'cause—"

"Unhand that woman!" demanded an imperious voice in answer to Jane's cry of distress, and a black-gloved hand intervened to break the offending grip of the offending hand and to knock it aside.

Jane turned to see her black-masked, black-costumed, black-caped deliverer who, rapier in hand, stepped valiantly to her rescue.

"Oh! *Senor Zorro*!" cried Jane. "My hero!"

Snatching with his free hand his other black glove from his belt, Jane's deliverer struck her would-be assailant across the mouth.

"Depart from this woman, or prepare to defend thyself!" he commanded.

"Uh—hey, Man!" said the wolfish-looking personage who resembled Donald, throwing up his hands. "I didn't mean no harm! No need to get sore!"

"Thou wilst not fight me, varlet?" said the Zorroesque figure. "Then, coward, bear my mark!"

So saying, Jane's deliverer with the point of his rapier cut a large M into the right breast of the varlet's black leather jacket—which Jane had not noticed until now he had been wearing.

"Hey Man!" cried the leering coward. "I just bought this jacket!"

"What care I, poltroon!" cried Jane's masked avenger. "Begone before I do worse to thee!"

Whereupon the leering, wolfish-looking poltroon turned tail and fled the dance floor.

Sheathing his rapier, doffing his black-plumed hat, clicking his heels and making a low, sweeping bow and kissing her hand, Jane's deliverer asked, "And now, *Senorita Juana Marguerita de Doe*, may I have the honor of this dance?"

"You have saved me," said Jane, "from a fate worse than death, *Senor Manuel Fernando de Ortega y Diaz de Rodriguez y Zorro*," for, seeing the thin, trim moustache beneath the lower edge of her rescuer's mask, Jane realized, as she extended her lovely hand for him to kiss once again the immaculately manicured tips of her long, slender, tapered fingers, that it was none other than he. "How can I refuse my deliverer aught?"

"Ah, *Senorita*, I am honored to have been able to render assistance to one so lovely! And may I say how absolutely alluring you look?" said her *caballero en mascara*. "And may I also compliment you on your most excellent taste in footwear?"

"Oh, *gracias, Senor!*" she said. "but what of the rest of my costume? Do you not think it very s—se—sex—very s—se—sed—seduc—very en—enti—very nice?"

"The rest of your costume, *Senorita?*" he asked, a puzzled look in his eyes.

Puzzled by her partner's puzzlement, Jane looked down at herself to discover that the sheer black negligee which only moments ago she had believed she was wearing was no longer there!

Quickly withdrawing her hand from her partner's, she protested, "You did that with your eyes, didn't you!"

"Not so, *Senorita*! You did it yourself. It is the sensual, passionate woman inside you coming out."

"Oh," said Jane. "Is that what it is? I was wondering. Well then, *mio Caballero*, now that I know, we might just as well dance, might we not?"

"Indeed we might, *mia cara Juana Marguerita*," said Manuel Fernando de Ortega y Diaz de Rodriguez y Zorro, and he folded her into his arms and swept her onto the dance floor.

With a start Jane awoke.

"Oh dear!" she cried. "I was dancing with him n—na—I was completelyn—n—nu—completely *en dishab—completement au natu—*I was utterly uncl—All I was wearing were my shoes! And—and I wasn't even embarrassed!" she exclaimed, horrified that she had not been horrified. "I was not troubled in the least to be dancing completely n—n—na—completely in the n—nu—totally uncl—like that—with Manuel Fernanado de Ortega y Diaz de Rodriguez! Oh dear! What is happening to me?"

Instinctively she felt under the covers and discovered that her negligee had ridden up past her b—br—brea—over her b—bo—bos—up to her arm pits.

"Oh dear!" she cried, striking her hand to her forehead. "Why have I allowed that man so completely to dominate my mind and influence my thoughts—to—to take possession of my soul? Oh me! Oh my! Oh deary, deary me! Heighdy! Heighdy! Misery me! Lackaday me! What is he doing to me? And how was it in my dream I could speak and think in Spanish, a language I've never studied?"

CHAPTER THE THIRD

Next day, Jane, still perplexed about the significance of her strange dream, paused outside the door before entering the Reading Room, uncertain whether she should have come to school with her hair falling to her shoulders in long, voluptuous tresses and wearing her red four-inch high heels—*ses chaussures rouges avec des hautes talons de quatres pouces.* (Jane fell quite naturally into French because it is, after all, the language of fashion, but just as she was perplexed by her ability in her dream to speak Spanish, a language she had never studied, so now she wondered how it was that she knew that what she wore on her feet were *su zapotos rojos con elevados tacons de cuatro pulgados?*) Her anxiety increased on seeing Manuel Fernando of the tripartite cognomen in a study carrel perusing a blue-covered volume.

—He's here again! she said to herself. Why is he always here when I am? Why can't he study somewhere else? But then, she reflected self-accusatorially, I could study somewhere else, such as at the Main Library.

Then, recalling that the significance of anything is never revealed until the last chapter, Jane screwed her courage to the sticking place and entered the Reading Room. To her surprise—and chagrin?—Manuel Fernando of the threefold surname did not so much as raise his eyes from the pages of E. K. Chambers's *William Shakespeare: A Study of Facts and*

Problems—a work indispensable to budding specialists on the Bard from Stratford-on-Avon.

—He's using the book I want again! Why does he always manage to do that? It's as though he knows ahead of time.

But again Jane reflected ruefully that she could as easily obtain the work from the Main Library, and so she selected, instead, the first volume of *The Variorum Spenser*, proceeded to a carrel as far away as possible from Manuel Fernando of the multilateral family name and immersed herself in the allegorical adventures of Una and her brave but immature champion Redcrosse Knight and of the machinations of Error and Hypocrisy. As she read, however, an unscholarly and unacademic thought kept nagging at her, and because she had a natural as well as an academically disciplined curiosity, she wondered why.

—He hasn't looked at me! Why? But then why should I care. He's nothing to me, after all.

She pressed on with her reading and note-taking.

—Perhaps he's at last getting the message that I don't appreciate his attention. But, she continued to cogitate Socratically, if I don't appreciate his attention, why do I wonder why he hasn't looked at me? But then, I suppose one always notices when a person departs from his or her normal patern of conduct. That, I'm sure, is what it is. Nothing more.

She pressed on in her reading of the adventures and misadventures of Una and her Redcrosse Knight.

—He certainly is very handsome, I have to confess, and I'm sure many a woman would be delighted at his attentions. If it were not for that smoldering passion in his eyes, those eyes that seem to undr—to str—to disr—to see me as though I were n—n—na—

"Hi Jane!" said a familiar female voice desturbing her wool-gathering.

Jane looked up to see the first both chronologically and alphabetically of her sextet of friends.

"Oh, hello, April."

"Coming to the Beer Garden at the Grad Centre this evening?" asked April with a friendly smile.

"Oh—uh—gee—I—I'm not all that fond of beer."

"Oh, but you don't have to drink beer especially," said April encouragingly. "You can get other drinks—just coffee if you prefer. Main thing is it's a great chance to unwind after a hard week of study and to meet people."

"Well," replied Jane managing a smile, "maybe I will."

"Great! Where will you be around four?"

"In the Reference Library doing some research."

"And what else would you do in the Reference Library? Goak here. This is writ ironic. Ha ha!" laughed April. "Okay. I'll meet you there with May, June, Julia, Augusta and Catherine."

"That's very kind of you, April—and of the others."

"*Nolo problemo*! And hey! We all like your hair like that! And wow! Those snazzy red high heels! Is there some special reason—or," she added with a glance toward Manuel Fernando of the trinary patronymic, "some special person?"

"Wha—? Oh. No—no special reason and certainly no special person. None whatever."

"You're blushing, Jane, and methinks," said April accusatorially, "thou dost protest too much, Ms Doe!"

"There's no one!" retorted Jane sharply.

"It wouldn't be—?"

"No!"

"You don't even know who I was going to name."

"It doesn't matter, because there isn't anyone."

"Okay, Jane, if you insist. I won't pry, but we'll all find out sooner or later. So, see you at four. Bye."

"Oh—yes—see you then. Bye."

And with a knowing smile and a wink, April tripped lightly away, leaving Jane wondering at whom she was most angry, April for her innuendoes or Manuel Fernando of the triple praedonymic for causing her to be so inwardly flustered. Resolutely she returned to *The Faerie Queene*, but just as Redcrosse Knight and Una were were about to enter the hovel of the wicked Archimago, a shadow fell across the page and the voice of him for whom Jane since her dream of the previous night felt so much apprehension spoke her name.

"Jane."

Reluctantly Jane tore herself from Spenser's romantic Faerie Land to stare into the present reality of the dark, passionately brooding eyes set in the arrogantly and aristocratically handsome, assertive, domineering face of Manuel Fernando of the triplicate patronymic—and probably, Jane seemed to remember from something she had read sometime somewhere about Spanish surnames, possibly a matronymic or two, as well.

"Oh," she said, feigning nonchalance. "Hello."

"*Buenos dias*, Jane," said Manuel, smiling graciously and bowing formally, though, Jane thought, not condescendingly.

—Perhaps his eyes are not so smoldering nor he so arrogant as I thought, mused Jane.

"Uh—*buenos dias*, Manuel."

"Ah! *Gracias*! But you said you did not know Spanish, Jane"

"Oh—no—I don't—not really. It's just that they always say '*Buenos dias*' in the old cowboy movies on television."

"Ah! To be sure. I used to enjoy them myself when I was a boy—a sort of secret vice. But Jane," he said, genuinely solicitous, "I just wanted to ask if you got along all right last night after I let you off downtown. I felt afterwards, what with the torrential downpour, that I should have waited and perhaps offered to take you to dinner and then drive you home. At least to drive you home."

"Oh—thank you," she replied, geuinely appreciative of his solicitude. "It's most kind of you to inquire, but I was all right. The rain let up while I was—while I was making some purchases—and I bought an—an umbrella—so I'll be ready for the next time it rains."

"A very wise move indeed. But, since I failed to offer you dinner last night, perhaps you would have lunch with me today?"

"Oh, you needn't feel guilty about last night. And—and thank you for your kind offer, but I have a meeting today at lunch, I—I was coopted onto the English Graduate Students' Council."

"Ah! Congratulations! You are becoming a very important personage. *Eh bien, peut etre un autre fois?*"

"Oh—uh—*oui—peut etre.*"

His French, Jane thought, probably because of his continental background, seemed very idiomatic.

"*Gracias, Senorita.*"

Spanish, she assumed, because it was his native tongue, he spoke perfectly idiomatically.

"*Auf wiedersehen,*" he said, with a formal bow and a click of his heels, and he turned and strode with his precise, measured, imperious and dignified tread from the Reading Room.

"*Au—auf wiedersehen,*" she called after him.

His German, she felt, was not as idiomatic as his French.

—He didn't even notice my new shoes! thought Jane ruefully.

* * * * *

Later, standing in one of the two lines at the bar in the Graduate Students' Centre—affectionately and anagramatically known as the GSC—with her friends April, May, June, Julia, Augusta and Catherine, Jane became aware that at the head of the other line stood none other than—as the knowledgeable reader of this kind of literature, if one can call it that, must surely have expected—Manuel Fernando of the extensive cognomen involved in an altercation with the bartender.

"*Sangre de Toro,* you dunce, not Sanka Coffee! What kind of bartender are you anyway that you've never heard of *Sangre de Toro*—the Blood of the Bull—a fine Spanish wine!"

"Uh—yeah—Well, like, I don't think we ain't, like, got none of that there. There ain't, like, been no call for it."

"Oh, you don't think you ain't got none of that there because there ain't been no call for it! That's because of the Canadian proletarian—not even bourgeois, but proletarian—preference for beer! Well, there's call for it now! Make sure you have it the next time I ask for it!"

"Okay, man, like, I'll do what I can, but like I said, there ain't, like, never been no call for it up to now—like. Can I, like, get you anything, like, else?"

"Well, might I be—like—expecting too much to ask for, like, a *Courvoisier* VSOP!"

"Coor—huh? We got, like, Coors Light if that's, like, what you want."

"That most certainly is not what I want! I said *Cour-vois-ier* V S O P!" thundered Manuel, emphasizing each syllable and letter for the edification of the hapless bartender. "It's a cognac, one of the very finest—which is probably too much to expect at this poor excuse for a *taverna!*"

"Uh—con act?"

"No! Not a con act! This travesty of a bar is the con act! A cognac—c o g n a c—cognac, a brandy! I don't suppose you ain't, like, got none of that there either!"

"Oh, brandy! Why didn't you, like, say that in the first place—like? Sure, we got brandy—but, like, just the house brand."

"All right! All right! I'll settle for that, though it's probably rot gut."

"Oh, like, it ain't bad."

"Well, let's, like, hope it ain't"

The harried, persecuted bartender turned to pour the drink only to find himself once more the target of Manuel's ire.

"You're not going to put brandy into an unheated glass are you! Where did you learn bar tending—the hockey arena! You put brandy into a heated glass, you jackanapes! *Santiago de Cordoba y Bilboa y Alicante y Cartagena y Burgos!*"

Finally getting what he wanted, Manuel Fernando and all that jazz stalked off to a corner to sulk by himself.

"Well!" exclaimed Augusta. "Who the hell does he think he is!"

"The nerve of the Iberian bastard!" protested Julia.

"Yes," said June. "What arrogant and unmitigated gall!"

"Thinks he's too good for us benighted Canadians!" said Catherine. "Why doesn't he go back where he belongs!"

"And good riddance too, if you ask me!" said Julia.

April, having already spoken at some length in this chapter, her comments are unrecorded, for this is an equal opportunity novel. Jane, however, wondered—somewhat to her own surprise—whether she entirely agreed with her friends' comments, particularly the last two by Catherine and Julia.

—Manuel was not very nice, but after all, she mused, the bartender was something of a dolt.

At that moment, Jane found that she had moved to the head of her line and was being asked by the more articulate second bartender, "What will it be, Miss?"

"Oh—sorry. A glass of white wine, please."

Seated, a few minutes later, with her friends and some of her friends' friends and a few of her friends' friends' friends, Jane, after introductions and the exchange of pleasantries, having hoped for a stimulating discussion of Donne's metaphysical imagery or the dramatic irony in *King Lear*, found herself instead listening to a litany of complaints about everything and everyone in the English Department from the personality of the Head and the candidacy examination requirement—Ron Harriott, already a few sheets to the wind, wanted to see the Doctoral Dissertation abolished—to the inadequacy of the TA stipends—general assent on that—to the cost of xeroxing and the color of the First Year English secretary's nail polish. Almost all of them were adamant that the Practical Criticism Examination, which all of them except Jane and—horror of horrors! Manuel Fernando de Ortega y Diaz de Rodriguez—had failed, should be abolished. Bored with this pettiness, Jane tuned herself out of the discussion and was sipping her wine and reminiscing nostalgically about simpler, happier, more idyllic times in Saskatoon—before she had met Donald!—when her reverie was interrupted by the sound of guitar—like strumming issuing from the upright piano.

—I know that music! thought Jane. It's "Anadaluza" or "Playera"—the Fifth Spanish Dance of Enrique Granados. Who could be playing it?

She turned to see.

—What! Manuel Fernando de Ortega y Diaz de Rodriguez a musician! And what a superb musician! In all my wildest dreams I'd never have thought him a musician—a matador, perhaps, but never a musician. And he plays like Rachmaninoff—well, almost like Rachmaninoff!

Indeed Manuel's fine hands stroked the keys, drawing throbbing, melodious sounds from the strings of the battered old upright. His head was thrown back, and his eyes were closed as though he drew inspiration from some invisible region, from some fifth dimension, some elysium, as though he were the medium through whom the music was communicated from on high to us mere mortals here on earth.

—Is this, wondered Jane, the same Manuel Fernando of the too many surnames who only minutes before had so mercilessly shent and scathingly berated the hapless bartender? How can such artistic sensitivity be reconciled with such arrogance? How can two such conflicting sensibilities live together in one human soul? Is he a man of many moods, of many facets, of deep complexity? Is he a man at war within himself, tormented by discordant and conflicting urges, pulled this way and that by clashing desires, a personality divided, a soul in torment? Have I, perhaps, been unfair to him? Have I misjudged him?

Absorbed in her reverie, Jane had not noticed Ron Harriott,* balding, pot-bellied, wrinkled, grizzled and bearded, known by his fellow students, because of his advanced years, as the Ancient Mariner, but who fancied himself still young in spirit, a rather indifferent scholar noted for his long, involved, complicated sentences, whose sole purpose in the Shakespeare seminar was to convince everyone, especially Jill Glover and Jana Ogimanieff, two of the prettiest young women in the class who always tried to sit somewhere else when he who fancied himself a ladies' man tried to sit beside them, that, because the concluding scene of the third act of *The Winter's Tale* was set on the sea coast of Bohemia and because the only time that Bohemia could have been said to have a sea coast was in the thirteenth century during the reign of Premysl Ottakar II who ruled from Silesia on the Elbe to Istria on the Adriatic, King Polixenes of Bohemia in the play was, in fact, Premysl Ottakar II, had risen and now many sheets to the wind, bombed out of his mind and drunk as a skunk, was reeling and weaving his way toward the piano.

"Shay, Ma'uel," he slobbered, "j'know 'I wa' hol' yer han' by th' Bea'les?"

"I most certainly do not!" snapped Manuel Fernando of the three part family name. "Why in the name of the Emperadore Carlos Quinto would I want to?"

---

*   Names have been changed to protect the innocent. (Ed.

"Hey!" driveled Harriott. "Sh'a real nize chune. Goesh li' thish."

While Manuel still played, Harriott with his bony fingers attempted to pick out the tune.

"Boor!" shouted Manuel Fernando de Ortega y Diaz de Rodriguez rising from the piano bench to his full six feet four inches or 190 centimetres. "Uncivilized, inebriate yahoo! I do not suffer fools gladly!"

Whereupon the haughty, aristocratic Spaniard elbowed Harriott on the chin, knocking him to the floor, and slammed down the keyboard cover on the drunkard's aforementioned bony fingers which still clutched the keyboard, and strode in high dudgeon and in furious, blazing choler, and mad as a boiled owl, from the Common Room and out of the Grad Centre.

"You know, that really wasn't very nice," a number of the people remarked on observing Manuel's behavior, but Jane stared after him in stunned, shocked, silent amazement. She felt annoyance with Harriott for breaking the spell, desecrating the moment of exaltation, savaging the interlude of rare sublimity and spoiling her enjoyment of the music. At the same time, she felt that Manuel had acted with unnecessary violence and ferocity, and in a pique of ill temper. Yet she had to admit that Ron Harriott was a thoroughly obnoxious and annoying ninny, and so she found herself tugged two ways: one part of her seethed with anger at Manuel's infernal pride, his Castillian arrogance and hauteur; the other yearned to follow him to pacify his fury, to calm his wrath, to still the tempest raging in his boiling, bloody breast, and perhaps cool him down a bit. How, she wondered, could one man so divide her soul? How could he, in the same instant, arouse in her bosom both anger and sympathy, vexation and compassion, hatred and—and—and—?

—Oh dear! Surely not the opposite!

Her bosom heaving with conflicting emotions, her mind battered to and fro between irreconcilable thoughts, like a galley charged with forgetfulness that thorough sharp seas in winter nights doth pass 'tween rock and rock, Jane, after an interval, so as not to encounter outside, or even worse, to seem to want to encounter outside, Manuel with the too many other names, set down her glass, rose from her chair, brushed back her golden locks, straightened her skirt, and, feigning an appointment, excused herself and left the Grad Centre.

CHAPTER THE FOURTH

When Jane checked her her mail box in the English Department office on the following Monday, she found, among the usual bumf, an envelope addressed, though in a firm, strong, bold, self-assured hand, simply "Jane." She opened it and read the following message written with many a flourish in the same firm, strong, bold, self-assured hand, to wit:

> Dear Jane,
>
> How deeply I regret that you should have witnessed mydisgraceful and unconscionable behaviour at the Graduate Centre last Friday evening. Oh, the curse of my Castillian blood! Oh that it might be calmed, cooled and allayed by your gentle and restraining influence! For your sake, Jane, I shall strive to be more temperate, to moderate my Castillian ire. Perhaps then you will regard me more favourably.
>
> Desperately, hopelessly, forlornly yours,
> Manuel Fernando de Ortega y Diaz de Rodriguez
>
> P.S. You looked absolutely stunning in your red high heels. May I suggest—and it will be, I promise, my last time—that you wear shorter

skirts to display to better advantage your lovely legs? Otherwise, the high heels fail to give their full effect.

In anguish Jane crumpled the note, tore it to shreds and threw it into the waste basket.

—Oh please, she cried to whatever powers might hear and aid her, help me! This is too much! I can't handle it! Please, Manuel Fernando de Ortega y Diaz de Rodriguez, leave me alone!

Then to her horror, she recollected that this was the day Manuel was to give his seminar paper on *The Taming of the Shrew* in the Shakespeare seminar. What would that arrogant, macho Castillian have to say about so controversial a play? She dreaded the thought of the possible sexist interpretation he might give it. At the same time, she felt pleased in spite of herself that he had noticed her red high heels and she did wonder whether, because she *did*, in fact, have very nice legs, perhaps she should wear shorter skirts—to please herself, of course, not Manuel Fernando de Ortega y Diaz de Rodriguez.

When the time came for the seminar, she arrived in deep trepidation and with a palpitating heart at the seminar room on the fifth floor of the Buchanan Tower. Pausing for a moment outside the door, she stiffened her sinews, summoned up her blood, disguised her fair nature with hard favored rage, screwed her courage to the sticking place—if the intrusion of a phrase from *Macbeth* into a quotation from *Henry V* may be permitted—and charged once more unto the breech, prepared—to intrude another citation from another play—to suffer the slings and arrows of outrageous fortune. That is, she entered the seminar room.

Manuel looked up at her as she entered.

"Hello, Jane," he said quietly, almost diffidently.

"Oh—hello," Jane responded, managing a wan smile.

He continued for some moments to look at her hopefully, but she said nothing more and quickly took her seat and busied herself with the text of the play and her notebook in preparation for the seminar as Manuel, looking somewhat downcast and crestfallen busied himself in turn with organizing his paper for presentation.

—I suppose, she thought, I should have said something to him, but at this moment, I don't know what.

Just then the professor entered, and, after the exchange of pleasantries, the seminar commenced. Rather to her surprise, Jane found Manuel presenting a scholarly and well reasoned paper in a calm and dignified voice, but then suddenly when he came to his conclusion, he launched into a completely outrageous peroration, though Jane's disciplined observant attention noted that he had not turned the page where she would have expected he should, and she wondered why. Probably, she reasoned, like many a student before him, he had been working on his paper right up to the last moment and had not been able to write out his conclusion. Yet, everything seemed too polished for extemporary remarks, but then, perhaps he was one of those who had everything composed in his head before writing it down.

"The whole play," he said, "comes a cropper at the end, the carefully laid structure comes crashing down, the meticulously laid plan goes awry, and our expectations are unfulfilled and ungratified. We expect Petruchio to remain strong," he continued, his tone objective and scholarly, "but instead, he caves in to Kate. He becomes too gentle with her, too generous in complying with her wishes, to indulgent in meeting her demands."

On the faces of everyone seated around the table, eyebrows rose quite perceptibly.

"Today," continued Manuel, "many—especially women—regard the play as sexist, but seen in the light of the era in which it was written, it is, in fact, far too liberal."

Gasps of shock and astonishment greeted that statement.

"Bear me out," said Manuel equably. "I believe you will find I can support my contention. Um—Yes—Where was I?" he said, his eyes scanning the page—the one Jane thought should have been turned. "Ah yes! That Petruchio yields far too readily and easily is strongly suggested by the experience of Hortensio and Lucentio with their apparently amiable spouses Bianca and the Widow, who, once married, show themselves all too soon to have been shrews under-the-skin, scheming women, one might almost say termagants, who had disguised their shrewishness, held it in check until they had entrapped their unsuspecting suitors. Kate, the formerly open and undisguised shrew has taken a lesson from them. She will pretend submission, she will feign docility, until Petruchio's guard is down, and then she will pounce. Fletcher's later play *The Woman's Prize, or The Tamer Tamed,* implies very strongly that Shakespeare's audience saw through Kate's sham. Petruchio ought to have maintained his dominance and his domineering stance, for Kate, as the examples of Bianca and the Widow demonstrate, is still a shrew at heart, like all women potentially . . ."

Again gasps of horror and cries of "Shame!" greeted that comment, but Manuel pressed on doggedly, making Jane, despite her deep anger at his stated sentiments, feel, nonetheless, a grudging admiration for his audacity.

"—a shrew at heart," Manuel resumed, "and totally incapable of change, for, as your own Canadian writer Davis Robertson says . . ."

"That's Robertson Davies!" interjected Jane angrily.

"Ah yes! Robertson Davies to be sure," said Manuel with and ingenuous and disarming smile. "Thank you, Miss Doe."

—Miss Doe? wondered Jane, puzzled and somewhat disconcerted by the sudden formality. Why now suddenly am I "Miss Doe" rather than "Jane"—or "Juana Marguerita"?

"As Robertson Davies," he said with deliberate emphasis, "has asserted, 'What is bred in the bone will out in the flesh.'"

—Hmph! thought Jane. He really likes that expression! He seems to think it accounts for everything, the . . .

But even in her mind Jane could not articulate what she considered Manuel Fernando de Ortega y Diaz de Rodriguez to be.

"Kate, I maintain," concluded Manuel, "is not tamed, and the only way open for Petruchio to keep her submissive would be to keep her barefoot and pregnant until she is completely worn out."

On the instant that Manuel Fernando of the triple-pronged surname dropped his bombshell—and laid down his papers—and before he could even sit back to await the explosion, the explosion occurred. Cries of "Sexism!" and even of "Fie!" "Horrors!" "For shame!" and "Oh!" burst from the throats of his classmates—including even the male members.

"Your basic assumption," protested pretty Jill Glover, "is that women are meant, even created, to be docile and subservient and that it is morally wrong for them to assert themselves. Well, that, *Senor* Ortega y Diaz de Rodriguez, is totally unacceptable!"

"From the point of view of your overly lax Canadian social standards that may indeed be true," said Manuel, like Tom Swift, quite good humoredly, "but that was certainly not the view of the Elizabethan Age when women were expected to be shamefast, and besides," he added with a smirk, "Natural Law dictates that women submit to men."

"Natural Law," remonstrated attractive Jana Ogimanieff, "is just a male chauvinist ideology to give moral and theological support for their historically conditioned position of dominance. It's nothing but justification of the status quo and a barrier to change and progress."

"You erroneously identify, if I may so, Miss Ogimanieff, change with progress," responded the completely unruffled Manuel. "As Alexander Pope says, 'Whatever is, is right.' More recently, women, seeing the privileges which men enjoy by virtue of their natural superiority, have been led to think that they deserve equality, just as, having had a glimpse of our standard of living, the peoples of the Third World—whom Kipling referred to as 'lesser breeds without the law'—originally quite happy with their lives, now want everything we have. Now that men have given women—quite mistakenly, I may say—a little bit of freedom and allowed them to enter the professions—a grave mistake—they now demand complete equality for which they are totally unsuited, and you do not have to look very far to see the disastrous results of this well meant but utterly misguided policy. Our whole society is in a terrible state of chaos—or chassis, as 'Captain' Jack Boyle says in O'Casey's *Juno and the Paycock*—uncertainty, disorientation and confusion."

—So, thought Jane, this is how he strives to become a new person! He, not Kate, is the one incapable of change!

Despite being impressed by Manuel's demonstrated knowledge of English literature, she could keep silent no longer.

"You say that," she expostulated, "because you come from a culture where women have always been kept submissive!"

"Ah, Miss Doe! There you are in error. During the Middle Ages Spanish society gave women a far greater degree of freedom and autonomy than anywhere else in Europe."

"Oh . . . ?"

"Ah yes! and I can show you studies—and not just by Spaniards—to support my contention. But," he said, with a mischievous twinkle in his eye, "we eventually saw the error of our ways and put women in their proper place."

"My point exactly!" exclaimed Jane. "Perhaps I was incorrect in my historical detail, but my over-all contention is correct, as you, in fact, have just admitted. Your society and culture oppresses women. But watch out! The winds of change have been sweeping into Spain since Franco left the scene!"

"Ah yes! I held no great affection for *El Caudillo*, but nevertheless the traditional values he upheld—undoubtedly too dictatorially and oppressively—are the right values. Revolutions, I fear, devour their children. Are people's lives improved by revolution? Look at Russia before the collapse of Communism. Does change bring greater happiness? Is it not definitely better to leave alone people who are content with their simple and humble lots than to promise them unattainable utopias?"

"Why then," demanded Jane, "if people are so happy and content in their poverty have they always demanded better conditions, equality of opportunity, basic human rights . . . ?"

"Too much misguided generosity," interrupted Manuel Fernando of the the three-piece cognomen, "too many concessions to the Third Estate—the masses, the peons, the coolies, the great unwashed, the sans culottes, the . . ."

"Reactionary twaddle!" shouted Jana Ogimanieff.

"Elitism!" cried Jill Glover.

"Fascism!" cried April, May, June, Julia, Augusta and Catherine in unison.

"Yes," interrupted the insufferable Ron Harriott, "but if we bear in mind that King Polixenes in *The Winter's Tale* is really Premysl Ottakar II . . ."

But as usual, no one listened to him.

Mild-mannered Professor Wordsworth Williamson tried manfully to break in and restore order to a situation verging on chaos—or chassis—and revolution and a possible lynching when Manuel Fernando of the triple-decker cognomen threw back his head and to the astonishment and consternation of all, roared with laughter.

"So!" he guffawed. "You've let the insufferably arrogant Castillian pull the rug over your eyes and the wool out from under you! You've let him lead you by the garden hose down the prim and rosy path to the

the dahlias! You've sat by while he burrowed below your pine trees and moistened you with your own petrol and blew you over the moon into a cock-eyed kettle of fish!"

A stunned silence greeted this startling and totally unexpected development—and the mangled cliches and quotations. Everyone stared at Manuel and then at one another, agog with wonder and dismay.

"Huh?" said someone.

"Perhaps," said Manuel, with his most engaging and ingenuous smile, "you would now like to hear my real conclusion."

—Wh—what? Thought Jane. So that's why he didn't turn the page! I should have realized there was something fishy going on!

Whereupon, turning over that very page which Jane had noticed he had not turned over, Manuel proceeded to read a reasoned, scholarly and balanced review of the divergent views of a number of feminist critics and concluded with one of them that because *The Taming of the Shrew* is, in fact, a play-within-a-play, it is not to be taken literally, but should be seen as in some sense a tongue-in-cheek utterance—"Rather like my earlier remarks," he interjected with a smirk, "a kind of ironically humorous slapstick farce."

—How infuriating! thought Jane after the seminar. The presumption! The effrontery! The unmitigated nerve and impudence of the man!

She collected together her books and rose from the table.

—Still, it was a rather good joke.

So musing, she left the seminar room.

—But he needs a short course in popular expressions and quotations—and perhaps a dictionary of slang and colloquialisms and a copy of Bartlett's Familiar Quotations.

Then, after leaving the campus, Jane found herself, for totally inexplicable reasons, going home by way of downtown where she stopped in at the Hudson's Bay Store and purchased a skirt which, if not quite a mini-skirt, was considerably shorter than anything else she had ever worn.

CHAPTER THE FIFTH

Lovely young Jane Doe sat sipping her Amaretto Almond coffee in Yum Yum's Cafeteria in the basement of the Old Auditorium where she had taken temporary refuge from her windowless office in the Auditorium Annex, finding solace in caffeine from the horrendously frustrating task of marking her first year English students' in-class essay analysis of a sight poem. Whether Manuel Fernando de Ortega y Diaz de Rodriguez would appreciate her in her new short skirt, her students certainly did, but that appreciation had done nothing to improve their writing or their understanding of literature. Were they all H*Y*M*A*N K*A*P*L*A*Ns, she wondered, for how else could they possibly have concluded that Shakespeare's sonnet beginning "Shall I compare thee to a summer's day?" was a patriotic panegyric celebrating England's victory over the Spanish Armada?

The horrors of the poor comprehension and the lack of language skills of her freshmen English students were as nothing, however, to a horror of another sort—her obsession with Manuel Fernando de Ortega y Diaz de Rodriguez. The more she tried to push him from her mind, the more he kept intruding into it, teasingly, temptingly, tantalizingly, tormentingly. Whenever she tried to relax to get away from her studies for a while, he would take possession of her imagination, and she would then reimmerse herself in her studies, only to have him trouble her sleep in strange and bizarre dreams.

Except in her graduate seminars she had spoken to him only once since his outlandish presentation on *The Taming of the Shrew*, and that in rather unexpected circumstances. The previous Sunday she had decided to attend the Church of St. Wilberforce in the Willows on University Boulevard in the Endowment Lands. She found the service to her liking, neither the dull-and-drab-to-the-glory-of God Low Churchmanship of a certain Eastern Canadian seminary which taught to aspiring candidates for the priesthood the faith once delivered to the saints in the sixteenth century, nor the exotic Anglo-Catholicism of that other Eastern Canadian seminary located across the street from the former in Toronto—does anything good come out of Toronto?—where aspiring young candidates for the priesthood were taught the faith once delivered to the saints in the twelfth century. As she left the church and after introducing herself to the rector, the Reverend Canon William Rowan, she heard from behind her a voice to which she had become more familiar than she wanted cheerfully calling her name.

"Jane!"

She turned to discover the speaker.

"Manuel Fernando de Ortega y Diaz de Rodriguez!" she exclaimed.

She assumed he had just arrived to attend the celebration of the Mass by the Roman Catholic congregation that met at St. Wilberforce in the Willows, and so she was taken aback by his next remark.

"How delightful to see that you are a fellow Anglican!"

"You—you are an Anglican!"

"Ah! I understand your surprise. It is not what one would expect of a Spaniard, and I am not strictly an Anglican but a member of the Spanish Reformed Episcopal Church which is incommunion with the Anglican

Churches, having received its orders from Anglican bishops—from the Church of Ireland, actually."

"Oh—yes—I've heard of it, but I never expected—I mean I never thought I'd ever meet one of its members here in Canada—or anywhere else, for that matter. It's very small, I believe—though of course, that's nothing against it."

"There are, indeed, very few of us, and I suspect you never expected the arrogant Castillian to be a member of it."

"I—I've never called you an arrogant Castillian, Manuel."

"But you have, perhaps, thought it? For I am an arrogant Castillian. But that is hardly apropos the matter at hand. The Church was organized by some Spanish Christians who dissented from the decision of the First Vatican Congress that the Pope was Infallible. My grandfather, who was a bit of an iconoclast and a nonconformist who had married a gypsy in defiance of his family, joined it almost immediately to flout them—a sort of nose-thumbing gesture, you might say—but very soon found himself committed, and his descendants, including me, have continued to belong to it and support it right down to the present. So here in Canada I attend the Anglican Church with which we are in communion. As with much else, Jane, it is an interest we have in common."

"Oh—I—uh—we—Well, yes—we do seem to have a few interests in common, but—but I'm sure we differ on many other matters."

"Ah yes! But difference makes life interesting! It is, one might say, the spice of life!"

And that was what so much troubled her now as she sipped her Amaretto Almond. The more she knew him, the more her suppositions about him were overturned and the more she found that she did have in common with him. It was all so very, very troubling. Surely she was not falling—!

"Jane?"

It was *his* voice interrupting her reverie! She looked up to see him standing before her. Was it mere coincidence, or was it fate that he should stand before her now, at this very moment when she was thinking such thoughts of him?

"May I join you?" he asked politely.

As she looked into his face she could not deny that it was an exotically handsome one, and to her surprise, the dark, brooding eyes no longer held their smoldering, haughty, arrogant, demanding glare, nor did they seem to be undr—looking at her as thought she were—well, you know how she thought they looked at her—but emitted instead a warm, humble, appealing glow.

Flustered, Jane replied, "Oh—I don't mind—I mean please do."

"Are you sure, Jane? You seem troubled—upset. I do not wish to—"

He seemed genuinely considerate and totally without the hauteur which had formerly characterized his approach to her.

"Oh—no. No, I was deep in thought—about the language problems of my first year English students, and—and—you—you took me by surprise. So—so, yes, please sit down—Manuel."

"Thank you," he said, seating himself across the table from her with with his cup of coffee whose aroma Jane recognized as Mocha Java, a flavor she herself often chose.

—Oh heavens! Is that also something we have in common!

"Ah!" he said as he seated himself. "I detect by its aroma you are drinking Amaretto Almond. That too is one of my favorites."

—Oh dear! Oh dear! What next!

"Do you mind if I smoke?" he asked considerately.

"Oh—!" Jane looked about her to discover that she had seated herself unwittingly in the smoking section. "No—no. Not at all."

"You're sure?"

How very solicitous he seemed of her ease and comfort!

"No—I mean yes, I'm sure. No, I don't mind. My father smokes a pipe."

"Ah!" said Manuel, producing an expensive meerschaum pipe from the pocket of his jacket. "Your father is a man after my own heart!"

Again Jane was taken aback, for she had expected that, as a Spaniard, he would smoke expensive Havana cigars, but instead, he smoked a pipe! But why on earth should it please her that, like her father, he smoked a pipe? She watched in fascination as he rubbed the rich tobacco in his hands, then carefully filled the bowl, and then tamped it in lightly but firmly—just as her father did!

—Any man who, like my father, smokes a pipe, she thought, can't be all bad!

And suddenly she found herself feeling more and more at ease with him—and with herself, and with the international situation, with the price of panty hose, with the T.A. union, and even, in fact, with British Columbia politics which, as everyone recognized, were so utterly hopeless that nothing could be done about them. A warm glow of absolute contentment came over her as she watched him strike the match, hold it to the bowl of his pipe, draw the flame down into the tobacco, and then puff out the smoke.

"Ah!" he sighed with satisfaction as he took a sip of his of his Mocha Java coffee. "Nothing like a pipe and a good cup of coffee!"

"Oh! That's what my father says too!" exclaimed Jane, a delighted smile wreathing her full, sensuous lips—though Jane would never have said that of them.

"I rather think I would like your father," said Manuel.

"He's a fine man," said Jane with pride as they gazed into each other's eyes.

"To have raised a daughter like you, he must be," Manuel said with obvious sincerity, and Jane blushed deeply.

"My—my mother also had a hand—a major hand—in producing and raising me."

"Ah! And I am sure she is a very fine woman. But Jane, how have you been this many a day?"

"I humbly thank you; well—well—well. And how, Manuel, have you been?"

"Well, too, I thank you—and busy."

"Yes, I'm sure. The life of a scholar is a very full one. I have been busy, too."

They sat in silence for some moments, gazing at each other.

"Your work is going well?" he inquired finally.

"Yes," she responded, "pretty well. And yours?"

"Quite well."

—We're each groping for things to say, thought Jane. Why are we so embarrassed?

"I thought," he said at last, "that you gave an excellent presentation on Donne's 'Songs and Sonets.' I really enjoyed it and learned from it."

"Oh, thank you. I—uh—I enjoyed your paper on *The Taming of the Shrew*," she said, hesitantly, remembering the great furor his paper had aroused. Then, seeing his smirk, and livening to the subject, she asked, "But whatever made you lead us down the garden path like that and make us all think you were a sexist reactionary?"

"Ah!" he said. "Precisely because that's what everyone did think of me—I rather think you have too, Jane—and I must confess that I've given good reason for everyone to think that of me, that I'm an arrogant Spanish *hidalgo* son of a—of a—well you know what they thought me a son of a, though I'm sure you would never have said so—and so, like Toad in *The Wind in the Willows*, I thought that I would give one final demonstration to satisfy everyone's perceptions, and then show that I have changed—and I have, Jane. I really have—at least I am trying to."

He looked deeply into her eyes as though seeking some sign of reassurance and encouragement.

"Oh—" began Jane as she remembered his note and felt very flustered, "I didn't—I mean you weren't—I don't think any of us minded—all that much."

"Ah! but everyone did mind—and you minded, Jane—and I came to mind myself. All my life I've been torn two ways, and coming to Canada with its big, open, friendly, easy-going welcoming heart—and meeting you—has shown me which way I want to go."

"Oh—well—I—You—we—uh—"

"I suppose," he continued, either ignoring or being unaware of Jane's confusion, or perhaps even trying to relieve it, "that it all has to do with my family history—this split personality of mine, I mean—but I don't want to bore you with that."

Jane's beautiful blue eyes looked into his darkly intense ones and read in them not only anguish but torture which told her of his need to talk, of his need for a sympathetic, understanding ear, and who, she asked herself, was she to deny him hers! Especially to a fellow Anglican—well, a member of the Reformed Spanish Episcopal Church in full communion with the Anglican Churches—who, like her father, smokes a pipe, who plays the piano like Rachmaninoff—well, almost like Rachmaninoff—who likes Shakespeare and Donne, and who, even though he can never get his name right, reads Robertson Davies!

"Oh no!" she exclaimed, with rather more enthusiasm than she had intended, "Manuel! I'm here! Do tell me—please! I am very interested!"

"You are most kind, understanding and sympathetic, Jane. I saw those fine qualities in you from the very beginning. There's not that much to tell, really, but you see, our family has been divided in its views and attitudes ever since the time of Napoleon."

"Napoleon?" said Jane, her blue eyes like limpid mountain pools, widening in surprsise.

"Yes, and as I am sure a person of your culture and learning, Jane, must surely be aware."

"Oh well," said Jane, blushing, "really I'm only—"

"Now Jane!" he admonished. "You are a cultivated person. I've been most impressed with your taste and erudition ever since I first met you. Don't be embarrassed by the truth, Jane."

Jane blushed even more deeply as Manuel continued, "You are well aware that Napoleon tried to bring Spain into his Continental System denying all of Europe the right to trade with Britain in the hope of bringing that nation to its knees; and, as he did with all the other territories he brought into his empire, he gave Spain, together with a new king, a more liberal and enlightened constitution and set of laws—the Code Napoleon than had been the case before. Alas! Unlike other parts of Europe, Enlightenment ideas had not penetrated very far beyond the Pyrenees and Spain rejected both king and constitution. Also the junta who directed the fighting against Napoleon—alas after their victory at Beylen they were always defeated, but they never surrendered—revived the Cortes—a sort of parliament—and promulgated a liberal constitution too, but on his restoration King Ferdinand VII rejected it."

"Fascinating!" said Jane, entralled. "But surely," she protested, "you don't approve of the nepotistic imposition of Napoleon's brother Joseph, a foreign monarch, on the Spanish people!"

"There you see, Jane. You are very knowledgeable. I doubt if many of our fellow students would have known that Napoleon had placed his brother on the Spanish throne or that his name was Joseph—or even that he had a brother."

"Oh—well—I—uh—I don't mean to show off—"

"My dear Jane! Sharing one's knowledge is not showing off! But in reply to your comment, no, of that I do not approve. I recount it simply as background. However, to return to topic, there were some, particularly in the region of Navarre, who did approve of Napoleon's reforms and those of the junta, and among them were some of my ancestors."

"Oh my!" exclaimed Jane, unaware that she had leaned toward him as she warmed to the story—or was it to the story's narrator? "How very interesting! That is indeed fascinating!"

"Well, yes—but when the French were driven out and Napoleon overthrown, reaction set in, and those who had supported the Corsican Ogre, as many thought him, found life a little too interesting—in the way the Chinese mean when they speak of 'interesting times'. As you perhaps know, among them to say, 'May you live in interesting times' is to utter a curse."

"Oh, yes!" she exclaimed. "Of course!"

"There again, Jane, you show your wide knowledge. But, again to my story. Ironically, when there was a liberal revolt against the reactionary King Ferdinand VII, it was a French army, under the authority of the Congress of Vienna, that entered Spain to suppress it. So, to make a long story short, my family has remained divided in its political opinions to this day. My immediate family were of the more conservative view, but when the Civil War broke out in 1936, my Grandfather, who was a brigadier general in the army, though he did not favor the Republic, nevertheless felt duty bound by his oath of allegiance to defend it against the Nationalists, as the rebels called themselves. That did not sit well with the rest of my family who hoped for a restoration of the monarchy—though, of course, in the immediate aftermath of the Civil War, they were disappointed, Franco merely making himself dictator—and *Abuelo* for a time became *persona non grata* among us, but when I learned his story, I came to admire him."

"He sounds like a man worthy of your admiration, Manuel," said Jane, beginning to see Manuel in a new light.

"Indeed he was."

"What became of him?"

"Well, after the fall of Barcelona in 1939, he and his troops fought a rear guard action to enable the many refugees—including the great Catalan cellist Pablo Casals—and the remnants of the Republican forces to get across the border into France, and he barely managed to escape into France himself where he was interned for a time, but when the Second World War came, he was allowed to join the French army. After the fall of France, it appears that he joined the Resistance, and then all trace of him was lost."

"Oh, I'm so sorry, Manuel!" she said, and, without realizing that she did so, reached across the table and laid her hand on his.

"You are *muy compasivo*—very understanding, Jane," he said, gazing tenderly into the clear depths of her beautiful blue eyes. "He was a man of honor, and I'm sure he died honorably, fighting for what he believed. But," he said, "I didn't mean to become so personal and to turn the conversation to such a sombre subject. And I have presumed too much on your good nature and taken far too much of your generously offered time."

"Oh, no, Manuel! I found your story very interesting and deeply moving. I really appreciate your sharing it with me."

"It was most kind of you, Jane, to let me do so and to listen so patiently, and I hope," he said, continuing to gaze into the azure depths of her sympathetic orbs, "that it has, perhaps, made you understand me a little better."

"Oh—yes—it has Manuel. I mean, we are all products of our histories and environments. Oh! That sounded so trite and stilted—"

"But true nevertheless, my dear Jane. I understand perfectly what you mean. But," he said, rising, patting as he did so, Jane's hand which had remained lying on his, "I must be getting along and let you return to your studies."

"Oh!—Must you?" She blushed on realizing that such a sentiment had so easily escaped her. Trying to recover her equilibrium, sang froid and poise, she stammered, "Uh—I mean, yes, I—uh—I suppose we do both have important things to do, but—but—I've enjoyed talking to you—Manuel."

She rose to leave the cafeteria with him.

"There's something I've been wondering about," she said as they walked to the door.

"Yes, Jane?" he queried eagerly.

"How is it that you have such a deep interest in English literature? In fact, you speak rather like an Englishman."

"Ah yes! I had an English governess and tutor, Miss Geraldine Fitzhenry—a most beautiful woman, by the bye—almost as beautiful as you, Jane—" he began as he held the door for her.

"Oh! I—I—" spluttered Jane, blushing for the fourth time in an hour.

"Yes, a beautiful, talented, cultivated young woman," he continued as they mounted the stairs to the ground level, "and it was she who introduced to the literature of her country for which she had a great love and understanding—an interest that has remained with me even after she ran off with my philandering Uncle Carlos"

"Oh! She ran off with your—!"

"Yes. No one could understand why. Well, certainly they could understand why *Tio* Carlos was interested in her. She was, as I said, beautiful and talented, but he was rather the *bete noir*—as you say, the dark ox—"

"The black sheep," corrected Jane.

"Ah yes! The black sheep of the family, and as I say, a philanderer, and Miss Fitzhenry did not seem the type."

"Perhaps," said Jane, rather to her own surprise as they reached the top of the stairs, "there was another more passionate woman inside her waiting to get out, and your uncle provided the opportunity."

"Wha—? Why, yes, Jane! How perceptive of you! Yes! And now that you mention it, I remember I used to see hints of that woman inside her—though at the time I was too young to recognize that that is what they were. Anyway, she seems to have had a good effect on *Tio*, for he seems to have renounced his philandering and remained faithful to her. The last we heard of them, they were living happily together in Montevideo, Uruguay."

Jane was silent for a moment as they stood facing each other at the head of the stairs. Then she said, "You—you come from a very interesting and exciting background, Manuel." Then she added, rather dolorously and ruefully, "I'm just and ordinary girl from a very ordinary background on the free, open, clean and innocent Canadian Prairies."

"Ah, but there must be something special and stimulating on those Prairies to have produced a woman like you, Jane!"

—He's flattering me, thought Jane. But no, no, it's just his way to speak effusively like that. And even if he is flattering me—I like it!

Aloud she said, "My Grannie—my maternal grandmother—has always maintained that I am related on her side of the family to the Duke of Argyle."

"Ah! There you are, Jane! Aristocratic blood flows in your veins! I knew you were someone special—though you'd be special even if there were not a drop of aristocratic blood in your veins."

"Well, I don't think the connection amounts to anything, really. His Grace has never been in touch."

"Ah! The arrogance of nobility! But, as I said, Jane, I must be getting along, or my papers will never be written."

"Yes, I know. There are always deadlines—one of the least attractive features of the academic life. I have papers to complete too—and student papers to mark."

"Then I must not detain you any longer, Jane. It has been a great pleasure talking to you."

"And—and I've enjoyed talking to you, too, Manuel."

"Well then, Jane, *hasta la vista*."

He smiled, touched his hat, and, meerschaum pipe smoking profusely, walked jauntily away and a sudden, deep and totally unexpected wave of disappointment flooded over Jane, and she stood in utter dejection as she watched him depart.

—Oh! He just turned and walked away! Why do I feel so devastated? I—I thought that he might have k—k—ki—ki—that maybe he would at least have tried to h—h—hu—hu—to em—embr—he didn't even offer to shake hands! Oh Manuel!

CHAPTER THE SIXTH

In her deep disappointment that Manuel had simply walked away without showing any sign of feeling toward her when she had been so overwhelmed by feeling for him, Jane returned to her windowless office in the Auditorium Annex and immersed herself in marking her English students' essays, doggedly persisted, and finished them late in the afternoon. Heaving a deep sigh, she rose from her desk, donned her coat and left the office.

—Perhaps, she thought as she walked disconsolately to the English Department Office to see if there was any mail, he doesn't like me all that much after all. Maybe he's just a gigolo, and I've been fooling myself all along in thinking he was interested in me. Well, why should I care. But oh! she sighed inwardly and very deeply. I do care! I do care!

In the Department Office, Jane found in her mail box an invitation from Alison, the Reading Room attendant, to a Christmas party in her overpriced, underheated, illegally maintained East Vancouver basement suite. Ordinarily Jane did not enjoy parties. Such gatherings, in her experience, where everyone sat around drinking beer and telling off-color jokes while the rock music, as the alcohol progressively deadened their hearing became progressively louder—boom boom boom boom bamma-bamma boom bam boom! Yamma-ramma yamma ya ya ya! Boom boom boom boom bamma-bamma boom bam boom! Yamma-ramma yamma ya ya ya! BOOM BOOM BOOM BOOM BAMMA-BAMMA BOOM BAM BOOM! YAMMA-RAMMA YAMMA YA YA YA! **BOOM BOOM BOOM BOOM BAMMA-BAMMA BOOM BAM BOOM! YAMMA-RAMMA YAMMA YA YA YA!**—(Why people played it at all, let alone so loud, Jane had never been able to understand)—represented the ultimate in inanity. However, she had visited Alison's suite on a number of occasions and had been impressed by the way in which she had transformed her hovel into a warm, cozy and tastefully cultivated habitat, and she knew, further, from Alison's always courteous manner and pleasant demeanor that she was a woman of refinement, and so she felt that for once she could a party with a distinct possibility of enjoying herself.

—Oh! she thought. Perhaps Manuel will be—But perhaps Alison didn't invite him. Well, why should I care!

But her effort not to care was unsuccessful, and she stole a peek into Manuel's file folder—because of his wealth he did not have to pay his way by being a Graduate Teaching Assistant and so did not have a box—and saw that yes! the bright green paper on which the invitation was printed was there!

—But perhaps he won't go.

Despite her doubts and fears, on the evening of the party, Jane took pains to look her very best—which was absolutely stunning—in a new green dress, the skirt falling to just above her knees, about her neck the pearls her parents had given her when she had received her M.A., and her gold four-inch high heels complimented by a gold handbag and a pin of gold holly and bells pinned over her left br—brea—on the left side just above her bo—bos—just below her left shoulder, all this finery made possible by the penetration of all the barriers to mail delivery raised by the inside workers of the Canadian Union of Postal Workers who played catch with parcels marked "fragile" and went on strike every time they suspected their salaries had dropped below those of university professors, by a letter from her parents containing another substantial cheque. (Jane excluded the letter carriers from her opprobrium, for she always found them very friendly and pleasant, likely to carry candies for the children and biscuits for the dogs on their routes.) Looking at herself in the bathroom mirror, a strange tingling sensation came over her, and she felt as though she were Cinderella, transformed into a glamorous princess by the magic of her fairy godmother, about to set out for the Prince's ball—though she was glad her slippers were not made of glass and, having paid a substantial amount for them, hoped she would not drop one on her way out. But then, she was under no obligation to leave by midnight.

But would Prince Charming be there?

Perhaps he wouldn't be, and if he were, would he simply ignore her?

Though her mood of elation collapsed as suddenly as it come upon her, Jane nevertheless set out to walk the short distance to Alison's suite.

And so, while in Canadian homes everywhere across this vast land, their Advent trees glowing in parlor windows, families seated themselves to watch American television programs, Jane, her mind a whirl of doubts and fears, set out for the party. It was a dark, stormy night—on the east coast of Newfoundland, but here in Vancouver it was a braw, bricht, moonlicht nicht, a lovely, balmy, warm, dry evening, the moon and the stars beaming down from a cloudless sky, a perfect night for romance if only there were someone—and not just anyone—to make it romantic. Would Prince Charming be at Alison's party? Would he be there?

Mind distraught, heart pounding, Jane arrived at Alison's domicile.

Alison met her at the door of her over-priced, under-heated but miraculously transformed—though still illegal—basement suite. From inside came the sounds of the guests chatting amiably and the baroque strains of a Vivaldi concerto—played, Jane could tell from the softer, less sharply focused string sound, on period instruments—from a CD in the stereo.

Jane thus found she had been right that this would not be the sort of typical party which she so disliked. In fact, this is probably unlike any party ever known to anyone. But this is a nice novel about nice people by a nice person for nice people. May they never perish from the earth!

"Jane!" cried Alison as her guest stepped through the doorway and removed her coat. "You look absolutely stunning!"

"Oh! Gee! Gosh!" said Jane, as usual flustered by compliments. "I just—well—thank you."

"Well, come in and let everyone see you!"

All eyes turned to Jane as she stepped into the large living room which ran the full length of the basement, and mouths dropped open, for indeed, she did look absolutely stunning, but Jane in her usual demure and modest fashion was totally unaware of the effect she was producing. Instead, she looked about her to see who was there and was happy to see April, May, June, Julia, Augusta and Catherine sitting together on one side of the room. She also noticed Ron Harriott and wondered how he had come to be numbered among the select group of Alison's friends, but perhaps Alison had been gracious and invited all the graduate students. But most important of all, she looked about to see if he was there.

He was!

A half-empty—or half full, depending on whether one is an optimist or a pessimist, of course—glass of a deep, red wine in his hand, he was standing in a far corner of the large room engaged in animated conversation with Jill Glover and Jana Ogimanieff, and on seeing him with these two very pretty young women, Jane experienced a moment of fear and jealousy, but then she noticed that Jill's and Jana's boy friends were standing near at hand. An empty chair was available right beside Manuel, and her first impulse was to rush over and seat herself therein, but remembering his rather abrupt departure from her after their meeting in Yum-Yum's, she restrained herself. Besides, though a simple girl from the free, open, clean and innocent Canadian Prairies, she had been raised, nevertheless, to behave as a lady, and a lady does not, most assuredly does not, make her desires and intentions obvious by acting impulsively but always with dignity and decorum. However, she did have to take her litre of *Liebfraumilch*—Jane had had to ask Catherine the meaning of BYOB on the invitation—to the table on which all the other contributions had been placed and right near where Manuel was standing, and so it was quite acceptable, because necessary, for her to approach him. And so, in her most lady-like manner, stately and with a simple dignity, ogled by all present as the most beautiful woman there—and perhaps anywhere—and to whispered accolades, Jane walked in her gold high heels toward the aforementioned table. At the very moment of her arrival at the table, Manuel looked up from his conversation with Jill and Jana and gasped in astonishment, his lower jaw dropping at least an inch, his eyes fairly starting from their sockets, as he beheld her radiant beauty so becomingly enhanced by her stunningly attractive attire.

"Jane!" he gulped, almost choking as he spoke, so overcome was he by the vision of Jane's grace, refinement and elegance. "You look gorgeous!"

"Oh!—I—uh—Th—thank you, Manuel!" she stammered, flattered, and blushed deeply in spite of herself.

Manuel asked to be excused from his conversation with Jill and Jana, who replied knowingly, "Oh, certainly, Manuel! We understand."

Manuel came immediately to her side and said, "You look utterly exquisite, Jane! Absolutely divine! Is that a new outfit?"

"Oh," Jane replied, trying to sound casual and off-hand, though in fact, she was all a-flutter inside, "it's just a little number I picked up the other day. Nothing special, really. I thought, since it's Christmas—well, Advent, really, but Christmas is coming—and for Alison's party—I mean, she has been such a good friend—so, well, you know, I wanted to—to—"

To herself she admitted that she wanted to impress Manuel, but she simply could not say so, after all!

Manuel came to her relief by saying, "Your taste is exquisite, Jane, and you wear clothes with distinction! It is you who complement the attire, not the attire you!"

Jane felt her face grow so hot that she thought she must look brighter than the lights shining on the Advent tree in the corner.

"Oh—th—thank you, M—Manuel. I—you—it—" she stammered, so unused to such flattery, such compliments that she did not know how to handle them.

"But I embarrass you, Jane," said Manuel, "though why you should be embarrassed by what is simply the plain, unvarnished truth, I cannot comprehend. But perhaps I might interest you in tasting a glass of Rioja?" he said, displaying a bottle of velvety red liquor. "Though I notice you seem to prefer a delicate white wine—most appropriate for a lady of your refinement, elegance and good taste—yet, I think you might find the full-bodied richness of this Spanish wine not unpalatable. Here," he said, pouring a small amount into a glass and holding it to her lovely, classic nose, "just savor the bouquet."

"Oh!" exclaimed Jane. "That is a lovely bouquet! And it does have a lovely, rich color!"

"Has it not? Would you, then, care to sample *un soupçon?*"

"Oh yes!" she exclaimed enthusiastically. Then thinking perhaps that she had displayed too much enthusiasm, she moderated her tone. "Why, yes, Manuel. Certainly. Indeed, I would be pleased to taste a little of it."

"Its flavor is best experienced and appreciated when it is poured over a slice or two of lemon or orange—or even some of each," he said as he dropped some slices of the aforementioned fruit into a glass and poured a rather generous soupcon of the wine over them. "One sips it to obtain the benefit of its full-bodied taste. But I need hardly say that to a woman of your refinement."

"Oh, well, I hardly—I just try to be nat—I—I mean my parents taught—Thank you," she said and received the proferred glass from his hand, but before she could place it to her lips, Manuel had raised his glass as though to propose a toast, which, in fact, he proceeded to do.

"To the loveliest, most beautiful, woman here—or perhaps anywhere," he said quietly but fervently, his deep, dark, handsome eyes glowing with romantic ardor, "to certainly the most beautiful woman I have ever known."

"Oh Manuel!" said Jane, blushing a deep crimson and dropping her gaze to the floor in her embarrassment.

"I mean it, Jane," he said, sotto voce so that there could be little doubt in Jane's pounding heart and reeling mind of the sincerity of his utterance. Indeed, as she timidly raised her eyes, themselves aglow with an ardor of affection she had never felt before, she saw that the old arrogance and the former hauteur were completely absent from his demeanor, manner and lineament. In fact, there was nothing of pride about him. His eyes glowed only with the ardor of love.

"Jane, I—"

"Yes, Manuel?"

But, as is usual at moments such as this in romantic novels, whatever Manuel intended to say remained unuttered, for just at that moment, their hostess, standing beside the baby grand piano, raised its keyboard cover and called out, "Manuel! Can we coax you to play for us?"

"Yes, Manuel, please do!" responded a chorus of voices.

"Perhaps," said Manuel, eager to return his attentions to the lovely young woman who lingered at his side and who had so captivated his heart, to Jane, in other words, "you would play for us yourself, Alison."

"I wish I could," said Alison, "but I can't play a note. I don't know one from another. I've only just inherited this piano from a misguided aunt who bequeathed it to me in her will. I was the poor dear's favorite niece, and she wanted me to have her most cherished possession, perhaps in the hope that I would learn to play—as some day I hope I may. But until then, Manuel, you are the most appropriate person to honor dear Aunt Matilda's memory. I've had it tuned especially in anticipation of your being here and in the hope that you would favor us with your brilliant pianism."

"Yes! Yes!" cried all the guests in unison—except one who, though she loved to hear Manuel play, longed earnestly to know how he had intended to complete his statement beginning "Jane, I—".

"Well," said Manuel, graciously condescending to the wishes of the assembled multitude, "since it's in honor of Alison's aunt—"

A burst of applause greeted his statement of acquiescence even before he could finish uttering it.

"I'm afraid," he whispered to Jane, "I must answer the call of duty, but I hope we may speak again later in the evening. There are things I simply must say to you, Jane."

"Oh—yes—I—You—I'll be here, Manuel. And—and I love to hear you play. You play like Rachmaninoff."

"Hardly that well!" he said. "But I appreciate the compliment!"

He bowed to her, took her hand in his and placed a kiss on the tips of her beautifully tapered and immaculately groomed fingers.

"Did you see that!" whispered one of the guests as Manuel turned to walk to the piano. "If he's not a man in love, I don't know who is!"

For the umpty-umpth time in less than an hour, Jane blushed, but, though, she was as surprised on this occasion as she had been weeks ago on the first occasion that Manuel had so taken his leave of her, she felt no revulsion, no inclination to mutter "Yech!" but instead a pleasant, intoxicating, tingling sensation throughout her whole being.

"I think there may be more than one person in love," said the aforementioned guest's companion casting an eye toward Jane standing dumb-founded in view of everyone.

While Jane stood thus bemused, Catherine called out, "Jane! Come and join us!"

And that, in the delirium of the strange, never-before-experienced emotions which she was feeling, Jane was only too glad to do.

At the same time, Manuel seated himself at the piano, flexed his fingers, cracked his knuckles and lowered his hands to the keyboard, but before he stuck a note, he spoke in a hoarse, husky voice so much in contrast to his former arrogant tones, and with a furtive, longing glance in Jane's direction, saying, "I dedicate this piece to the loveliest lady I know."

All eyes turned toward Jane who sat blushing in her finery, and April, May, June, Julia, Augusta and Catherine asked rhetorically, since they all intended to concentrate on rhetoric in the second term, "Now I wonder who that might be?"

Jane, forgetting Manuel's advice and her lady-like upbringing, to try to calm her emotions, took a rather too large gulp of her *Rioja* and choked on it, prompting April, May, June, Julia, Augusta and Catherine to pat and stroke her vigorously on the back. Meanwhile, the strains of Liszt's *Liebestraume*, beginning softly, then rising in intensity, sang forth from the piano, coaxed from the taut wires of the instrument by Manuel's loving touch on the keys.

—*Liebestraume*! thought Jane, having somewhat recovered her composure. "Love's Dream!" Oh Manuel!

Eyes fixed always on Jane, Manuel's fingers nevertheless unerringly found the right keys as, with the brilliance and musicality of Rachmaninoff—well, almost of Rachmaninoff—he poured his soul into the music, gently stroking and loving caressing the keys and then with passion and power as the music rose in intensity toward the climactic cadenza—the nemesis of many a lesser pianist, but under Manuel's talented fingers executed flawlessly, brilliantly, passionately—and then returned the music to its original theme with an intensified ardor before bringing it back to its opening mood of hushed tranquility, the final phrases almost inaudible. His audience sat or stood in awed silence for several moments, overcome by the artistry of his playing before breaking into thunderous and enthusiastic applause which seemed to awaken him from a trance. He rose from the bench and acknowledged the ovation with and appreciative bow and was about to leave to return to where his heart called him, but cries of "More! More!" "Encore!" "Please don't stop now, Manuel!" forced him to seat himself again at the keyboard.

Reluctantly, yet graciously, it seemed to Jane as she peeked up at him, Manuel seated himself once again at the keyboard. Again giving Jane an ardent glance which once again set her heart aflutter and caused her to blush, Manuel began to play Rachmaninoff's transcription of Fritz Kreisler's *Liebesfreud,* "Love's Joy," and again all eyes turned toward Jane, but she, torn between embarrassment and joy failed to notice. Again he played both brilliantly and ardently, yet with that lofty patrician artistry which characterized the playing of the transcriber and which Jane now recognized with equanimity was so suitable to his own character. If the intention of the music was, as Beethoven had said, that heart should speak to heart, then it was certainly speaking to one heart.

Again as the last notes died away and the applause broke out, Manuel rose from the Steinway as though gripped by an urgent wish to return whence he most desired to be, which Jane fervently hoped and believed was by her side, but again the assembled guests refused to allow him to do so, and again he seated himself at the keyboard to play Carl Maria von Weber's "Invitation to the Dance" through which the congenitally lame composer had expressed to his wife who loved to dance both his regret at his inability to dance with her and his deep desire to be able to. Again the choice of music seemed suggestive, and Jane felt herself swaying in time to the waltz rhythm of the piece's central section depicting the dance of the cavalier with his lovely partner, and she imagined herself in a gorgeous gown of red brocaded silk swirling in the arms of Manuel Fernando de Ortega y Diaz de Rodriguez in the costume of a Castillian gentilhombre—close-fitting jacket and shirt with ruffed front and cuffs, tight fitting knee breeches, long white hose and black pumps—on the floor of the great baroque sala of a casa in *Espagna*—if only the music were not written with a Viennese ballroom in mind.

All too soon the music concluded, bringing to an end her dream, but Jane hoped that now at last that Manuel—though she did love to hear him play—would be allowed to return to her side, but as the applause broke out once again, the doorbell sounded, and Alison ran to answer it.

"Is this an exclusive party," a female voice rang out, "or can a refugee from the frozen wastes of Siberia crash it."

"Yvette!" cried Alison. "Yvette la Flambee!"

"Oh-oh!" cried Augusta. "Hang onto your boy friends, ladies! The Panther's back!"

Jane did not like the sound of that admonition at all!

Alison meanwhile had stepped aside to permit the entry of a stunningly glamorous, dark-haired, creamy complexioned young woman in a fabulously expensive sable coat, her hair combed with seductively artful nonchalance over her left eye.

Why is it, Jane wondered, that at the very moment when the heroine is falling in love with the hero, romantic novelists inevitably introduce a potential rival and inevitably *une femme fatale*?

"Look who's here!" said Alison. "It's Yvette back from her leave of absence to model furs in Siberia. And Yvette! What a gorgeous coat!"

"It is rather nice, isn't it" said the exotic newcomer, pulling the collar up about her neck and stroking the fur. "It's a gift from Vladimir and Lyudmilla."

Yvette paused to allow the bombshell she had just dropped to explode. A stunned silence ensued, no doubt as she had intended it should, as everyone looked questioningly from one to the other in astonishment and whispering "Vladimir and Lyudilla?"

"Putin, of course," said La Flambee with contrived casualness as she slipped off the coat and with calculated insouciance draped it over the back of a chair so all could admire her in her black strapless party dress with its very, very short skirt, her black patterned nylon hose, and her very high five inch—or 12.7 cm.—stiletto heels. Everything about this glamorous newcomer, despite her affectation of casualness, was, in fact, all too veddy veddy *soignée.*

Why, wondered Jane, do potential rivals always have to look like that!

"You don't mean," began Alison, responding, probably as the glittering newcomer had hoped to the contrivedly casual bit of name dropping, "surely you don't mean . . ."

"Oh indeed yes!" broke in La Flambee. "The President of Russia himself and his attractive wife just happened to be in Novosibirsk when I was modeling there and Lyudmilla came to my show and no sooner had she seen me modeling a coat like this that she just knew she had to have one and when Vladimir and his entourage came to pick her up she persuaded him to buy it for her so when you see a picture as I'm sure you will some day of Lyudmilla Putinova in a sable coat just remember that it was because I modeled it that she obtained it."

"The President of Russia bought the coat for his wife!" exclaimed Alisom. "I thought he could simply have it for the taking."

"Oh no, my dear!" said Yvette with a toss of her head—a toss which seemed, briefly, to indicate that she did have two eyes. "Vladimir is very particular that in the new Russia high political rank should not confer special privileges not even on the President and his attractive consort and then when he heard that I was in Moscow to give my show he sent a messenger to my suite at the Moscow Marriott who knocked on my door even while I was unpacking my things and I went to answer it and whom should I see there but a perfectly darling Colonel of Militia with a large package under his arm and an envelope in his hand who saluted and asked in just absolutely impeccable English if I were Comrade la Flambee imagine that Comrade al Flambee me and well of course I said that I was and he extended me the envelope and asked if he could place the package on the sofa for me and of course I said yes and he told me it was from the President of Russia and his wife and then he asked if I were free for the evening for he believed the envelope contained an invitation to the evening's performance at the Bolshoi Theatre and if it were an invitation and I were free then he the Colonel was to be my escort and the President and the First Lady would like an immediate reply and I opened the envelope immediately and indeed it was an embossed invitation from the President and the First Lady of Russia requesting the honor of the presence of *Mademoiselle* Yvette la Flambee in their box that evening at the Bolshoi for a performance of Swan Lake and of course I told the handsome Colonel of Militia that I would be delighted to accept the kind invitation of the President and the First Lady and would he convey to them my most profound gratitude and then I opened the package and what should I find in it but this very coat with a card saying 'To Comrade Yvette la Flambee from Vladimir and Lyudmilla Putin' and I almost fainted on the spot when I saw it and cried out in sheer and utter delight and told the Colonel to convey my deepest thanks to the President and his wife for such a lovely gift and what time would he be coming by to escort me to the Bolshoi for I would be just delighted that he should be my escort and since we would be spending the evening together might I not know his name and he said '*Da,* Comrade I am Comrade Colonel Sergei Alexeivich Timoshenko and I will call for you at seven-thirty Moscow time' and I said I really looked forward to going with him than and that I would be ready when he arrived."

"My goodness!" exclaimed Alison. "what a delightful experience that must have been!" while Jane wondered how this dark-haired, creamy skinned egotist could talk at such length without punctuation.

"It was an absolutely delightful evening!" Yvette gushed in response to Alison. "And dear Sergei Alexeivich looked so absolutely stunningly handsome in his dress uniform and was just absolutely infatuated with me and I must say that I did look quite stunning in my red dress with red shoes and red handbag and red gloves for well I know Communism has fallen in Russia but red is still a very popular color there and red just seemed so appropriate and when I got back home to Vancouver I found a letter from Sergei telling me how absolutely stunning I looked and really I do look so utterly fabulous in red and could he hope that I might condescend to let him correspond with me and of course I wrote back immediately to tell him that of course he could I mean what am I to think a Colonel of Militia just dying to have a relationship with me and Oh! who is that absolutely divinely handsome man sitting at the piano and was it he I heard playing as I came to the door?"

Jane's heart skipped a beat on hearing, as she feared she would, Yvette expressing an interest in Manuel—her Manuel!—and she noticed that Manuel's interest, like everyone else's, had been fixed on the fascinating and glamorous intruder.

"Oh," said Alison, "of course, you don't know Manuel. He's new to our midst—all the way from Spain." And Alison proceeded with introductions. "*Mademoiselle* Yvette la Flambee, *Senor* Manuel Fernando de Ortega y Diaz de Rodriguez."

In her twelve and seven tenths centimetre high heels, Yvette minced and teetered across the room, and Jane wondered how she managed to avoid falling flat on her face and an another part of her anatomy, especially the other part of her anatomy which made her look somewhat top-heavy. Jane had always thought—in private and somewhat to her embarrassment—

that her br—her brea—her bo—her bos—her thoracic development was quite nicely advanced—not too advanced but still perhaps a little more nicely advanced than that of many a young woman—but this woman's thoracic development was utterly—well—extravagant.

As she approached Manuel, Yvette held out her hand as though expecting Manuel to kiss it.

—Oh please don't kiss her hand, Manuel! cried Jane to herself in anguish. Your lips should touch only my hand, never another's—and certainly not hers!

"Absolutely delighted to meet you, Senor!" gushed Yvette. "I just love Spain. Majorca is absolutely divine! Have you ever been there?"

"Many times, Mademoiselle," said Manuel, rising courteously. [Oh Manuel! thought Jane. Can't you ever be a boor occasionally?] "My family owns a villa there."

"A villa on Majorca oh how fabulous and was that you I heard playing the piano oh so absolutely divinely as I came up to the door?"

"It was I who was playing the piano, Mademoiselle," he said, and Jane was deeply gratified that he showed no sign of appreciating her effusive compliment.

"Oh my and you play just utterly divinely like—like—like Liberace."

Manuel Fernando de Ortega y Diaz de Rodriguez winced and affirmed with great resolution, "I should hope I play better than that, Mademoiselle!"

—I knew he wouldn't receive that as a compliment! thought Jane, greatly relieved at his cool response.

"Oh!" said Yvette la Flambee, rather taken aback by the rebuff. "What I mean is that you play absolutely wonderfully—better than nanyone else I've ever heard!"

"Mademoiselle is most kind," said Manuel formally and rather coolly, but still, Jane noticed, he could not keep his eyes off the glamorous intuder.

—Oh that Judas! she thought. He has taken her hand. If he kisses it, I'll never—Oh! No! he hasn't kissed it, but he's bowing to her courteously—even if formally—and he's undr—he's looking at her as if she were n—n—nak—he's seeing her as though she were not w—wearing anything—but then, that outfit of hers rather encourages one to look at her like that—but the only one he should be looking at like that is—Oh good gracious! What am I thinking!

With all this happening before her eyes, Jane thought she had better get over to Manuel as quickly as possible. However, as she rose from her seat, Ron Harriott, drunk as usual, presented himself before her and blocked her way.

"Well, hi there, Zhane!" he slurred.

"Oh, hello, Ron. Look, I have to—"

But he grasped her by the arms and said, "Yer looghing ver' nize, t'nigh', 'f I may shay sho, shpecially in thoshe high heelsh. Maig y' loog ver' zegzy."

"Oh—well—Look, Ron, I really must—"

"Y'know, I gould reall' go f'r a girl li' you. Tha'sh a real grea' bair 'eadligh's y' go' there, y' know."

"Headlights?" queried Jane, perplexed.

"Sure. Y' know, knoggers."

"Noggers?"

"No' noggers, knoggers."

"Oh—knockers. Knockers?"

"Yeah, Y' know, 'oodersh—boobsh—Theesh things," he said, poking his fingers with unashamed effrontery into Jane's much, if modestly, prized thoracic development.

"Now you watch yourself, Ron Harriott!" Jane protested vehemently, pushing his bony hand away. "You keep your fingers to yourself!"

"Shorry," said Harriott. "Di'n mean any ovvensh. Jus' wan'ed t' maig a boind."

"Well, make your points elsewhere and about something else!" retorted Jane Doe forcibly.

Just then, Alison, who had moved over to the CD player, called out as she prepared to insert a disc, "Time to dance, everybody. I've had the rug rolled back away at the end of the room, so everyone find a partner!"

—Oh dear! I've just got to get away from Harriott! thought Jane, despairingly. Do I have to dance with this besotted and inebriated nincompoop while Manuel dances with that—that meretriciously exotic and glamorous tart!

She tried to see around Ron Harriott, but he kept moving to block her view, so that she could not discover if Manuel had selected Yvette as his partner—or that Yvettte had inveigled him into selecting her. She feared the worst.

Harriott seemed not to have heard the announcement.

"Nize shtring o' beads," he said, admiring Jane's necklace.

"They are not beads!" protested Jane vigorously. "Now if you'll excuse me—"

"Hey! Whasha hurry?" protested Ron Harriott drunkenly. "They're no' real bearlsh, are they?"

He stretched out his bony hand to try to grab the necklace, but just as Jane raised hers to strike his hand aside, another hand, swarthy complexioned but extremely fine, intervened to grasp Harriott's boney wrist.

"You've a way of getting your hands in where they are not wanted, haven't you, Harriott?" said Manuel Fernando de Ortega y Diaz de Rodriguez in a calm, cold and level but menacing tone.

Jane turned to Manuel in both surprise and gratitude.

And, as she had in her dream, she exclaimed, "My hero!"—though unlike in her dream, Manuel was not dressed as Zorro, and she was not n-n-n—she was not un—uncl—she was now most elegantly attired.

"Washa gonna do, Ma'uel?" demanded Harriott. "Shlam a biano lid dow' on my fin'ersh agai'?"

"No, but I shall do worse if you don't step aside and let me dance with Jane."

—Oh! exclaimed Jane to herself, clasping her hands together. He *does* want to dance with me!

"Danze?" queried Harriott. "We gonna danze? Howja know I do'n' wanna danze wiz Zhane?"

"The question is not whether you want to dance with Jane, but whether Jane wants to dance with you! Perhaps we should inquire of the lady. Jane?" asked Manuel Fernando de Ortega y Diaz de Rodriguez. "Do you wish to dance with this gentleman?"

"No, I most certainly do not!" asserted Jane Doe firmly.

"So blow!" said Tom Swift breezily as he wafted by and overheard.

"Indeed," said Manuel. "For all our writers do affirm that ipse is he. Now you are not ipse, for I am he."

"Whish he'sh 'at, Ma'uel?"

"He, sir, that shall dance with this woman. Therefore, you clown, abandon (which in the vulgar is leave) the society (which in the boorish is company) of this female (which in the common is woman), which together is abandon the society of this female, or, clown, thou perishest; or to thy better understanding, diest; or, to wit, I kill thee, make thee away, translate thy life into death, thy liberty into bondage. I will deal in poison with thee, or with bastinado, or in steel; I will bandy with thee in faction; I will overrun thee with policy; I will kill thee a hundred and fifty ways. Wherefore, tremble and depart."

"Do, good Harriott," said Jane.

Harriott looked from Manuel to Jane and back to Manuel again, said, "Oh!" and trembled and departed—where to, no one has ever been able to discover, for he does not appear in this novel again until the very end.

Manuel thereupon offered his arm to Jane and walked with her to the dancing area.

"Who's that!" hissed Yvette la Flambee as Jane, ignoring her rival but looking happy and unashamedly triumphant, walked past her on Manuel's arm.

"Why," said Alison, "that's lovely young Jane Doe from the free, open, clean and innocent Canadian Prairies who has come to do her PhD at the vast, intimidating, intellectually over-sophisticated campus of the University of British Columbia here in the sprawling, worldly wise—and perhaps just plain worldly—slightly decadent, perhaps even somewhat wicked, but gorgeously situated and rather exciting west-coast city of Vancouver. Manuel Fernando de Ortega y Diaz de Rodriguez from Spain seems quite taken with her—smitten, in fact."

"Hm!" said Yvette, her green, snake-like eyes narrowing—or at least the one green snake-like eye that could be seen narrowed. "We'll just have to see about that!"

On the dance flour, Manuel said, "You dance divinely, Jane!"

"That's because you give such a wonderful lead, Manuel," said Jane, her full, red lips smiling up at him, her eyes sparkling brightly.

"Ah Jane! As always, you are too modest—though it is a most becoming and charming characteristic in you. You know that you are the most beautiful woman here—the most beautiful I have ever met anywhere?"

"Oh? And what," asked Jane, her jealousy getting somewhat the better of her, "about Yvette la Flambee? You were certainly giving her the eye!"

"Ah yes. Somewhat exotically glamorous in her cheap, sleazy, meretricious way. Attractive at first glance, no doubt, but it's all surface glitz. What you see, is all there is. You, Jane, on the other hand, are the real thing, the unalloyed gold, the unvarnished original, *la fine fleur de farine, comme disent les Français*, the rose which is a rose which is a rose, as Gertrude Stein so effectively put it in her most inimitable fashion, that perfect summer's day extolled by the poet and that gem of purest ray serene extolled by the other poet—the very quintessence of beauty. You, Jane, as Browning's Andrea del Sarto said, are the thing—the *sine qua non*, the *ne plus ultra*."

"Oh Manuel!" exclaimed Jane. "You say the nicest things. But—but would you really have kissed her hand which she extended to you and you took?" she asked, wishing even further assurance.

"Never!" he affirmed resolutely. "From this day forward, no hand but yours shall ever feel the touch of my lips—except perhaps my dear mother's!"

"Oh Manuel!"

"But," said Manuel, beginning to recognize that this chapter was becoming far too saccharine and sentimental, it's language too flowery, "let us leave the uninteresting subject of Yvettte la Flambee and talk of a far more interesting one of Jane Margaret Doe."

"Oh Manuel, I'm really not very interesting—only a little Prairie flower, perhaps a crocus."

"Ah Jane! You must stop belittling yourself and recognize that you are as most remarkable young woman—intelligent, cultured, well-mannered, refined, cultivated, and as I have said, very, very beautiful."

"Oh—oh, thank you, Manuel," said Jane blushing in her finery. "And you are very, very handsome—the most handsome I have ever met. I could not imagine anyone more handsome!"

"From you, Jane, that is a surpassing compliment, the greatest I have ever received!"

And to Jane's amazement, Manuel Fernando de Ortega y Diaz de Rodriguez blushed; he actually blushed!

"It's true, Manuel," Jane reassured him. "You are the most handsome man I have ever known—or—or ever hope to know!"

"Why Jane!"

He drew her very close to him—pressed her against his manly breast in which his heart beat amorously, and for some moments, the whole assemblage turning to notice—Yvette la Flambee's one visible green eye becoming even greener with envy—they danced in silence.

"You know, Jane," whispered Manuel, romantically breaking the romantic silence, "that I love you."

"Oh Manuel, I hardly—"

"I know I've behaved in an abominably arrogant manner toward you, Jane, so I know that your feelings toward me must be—it must be very hard for you to—Jane! Because of you I am a changed man! Please, Jane, dearest! Please give me a chance to prove—to deserve to—!"

"Oh Manuel!" she protested. "I've not always been nice to you. You're just not like anyone I've ever known before, and I've not always understood you, but—but I—I—l—lo—love you too, Manuel!"

Immediately he stopped in his tracks, drew her close to him—even closer than he already had—and to the "Oohs!" and "Ahs!" of the assembled multitudes—and to the sound of Yvette la Flambee grinding her teeth—he placed a long, lingering, passionate kiss upon her lips.

"Manuel!" exclaimed Jane. "In front of all these people!"

"Just observing a fine old English custom, Jane."

"Taking advantage of an innocent defenceless, vulnerable and unsuspecting young woman from the free, open, clean and innocent Canadian Prairies to kiss her in public is a fine old English custom, Manuel?" asked Jane, deeply embarrassed. "I always thought them a rather reserved people."

"Another ethnic stereotype. But Jane! It is the Yuletide. Look above you," he said, raising his eyes to the ceiling—or so Jane thought until she did look above her and in the direction of Manuel's eyes to see hanging from a light fixture immediately above her head a sprig of mistletoe.

"Oh!" she exclaimed. "Oh Manuel!"

"You see! *Feliz Navidad*, Jane dearest! Merry Christmas!"

"Oh yes!" she whispered. "*Feliz Navidad*! Merry Christmas, Manuel—darling!"

CHAPTER THE SEVENTH

Manuel, aglow with romantic ardor, suggested to Jane that they leave the party in Alison's over-priced, under-heated apartment—with all the people present the latter quality had not mattered, and was, in fact, an advantage—early, and Jane, equally aglow with romantic ardor had eagerly agreed, yet found her eagerness a bit disconcerting, wondering at its motivation. And so, with Yvette la Flambee glaring at them through narrowed eyes—at least the eye not hidden by her hair was narrowed and glaring—Jane and Manuel thanked Alison for her hospitality as whispers of "I wonder where they're going!" and "I wonder what they're going to do!" buzzed through the assembled guests, and Jane found herself also wondering what they were going to do—what Manuel was going to do and what she herself wanted to do if he did whatever it was he was going to do!

And so they stepped out into the night, Jane's right hand held tightly in Manuel's left through which contact the powerful effect of his intense masculinity sent electric shivers through her whole frame so that she wondered whether she were, in fact, the heroine of a polite, genteel novel, or if she were rather the heroine of a torrid, passionate, steamy romance, and she found herself, somewhat to her dismay, almost hoping that perhaps it was the latter.

And perhaps, for all Jane knew, her intense femininity was sending electric shivers through Manuel's whole frame so that he too wondered into what kind of novel he had been led by falling in love with this lovely young woman from the free, open, clean and perhaps not so innocent Canadian Prairies.

Oh Jane! Have I been mistaken in my heroine? Does a wanton, passionate voluptuary lurk within that seemingly demure and innocent breast waiting to be released? And you, Manuel Fernando de Ortega de Diaz y Rodriguez, are you the man who will release that hidden woman? Alas, at this stage I cannot tell and can but wait for my muse to guide me.

At the moment, Manuel simply asked in his most polite and gentlemanly manner, "I hope, dearest Jane, that I may have the privilege and honor of driving you home?"

And Jane, in her most lady-like manner, responded, "That's very sweet of you, Manuel, darling. I should be very happy to let you drive me home."

And so he led her to his opulent red Lamborghini and opened the door for her to enter.

Her eyes sparkling more brightly than the myriad stars that did shine and twinkle on the Milky Way above the Lower Fraser River Valley, Jane smiled up at him as she seated herself and murmured, "Thank you, Manuel."

When Manuel had seated himself beside her on the driver's side, he did not immediately start the engine, but took her into his arms, drew her very close to him, held her tightly against his broad manly chest, and kissed her long hard and passionately, kissed her, Jane knew, as no other had ever kissed her, a kiss that was like fire or strong, rich, heady wine—*Rioja* in all probability.

"Oh Jane!" he sighed deeply and heavily, a sigh so piteous and profound as it did seem to shatter all his bulk. "Oh Jane, my darling! How I have longed for this moment!"

"Oh Manuel!" sighed Jane equally deeply, heavily, piteously and profoundly—but one would hardly describe Jane's lovely, shapely figure as bulk. "How I have longed for this moment too—but I was far too stupid to realize that I did. Can you forgive me for being so obtuse?"

"Oh, of course, my darling! Can you forgive me for being so arrogant as to think that all I had to do was look at you and you would fall head over heels in love with me?"

"Oh Manuel! I almost think that I must have done so, for why, otherwise, have you been such an obsession to me? I realize now that that I've been fighting my own heart."

"Well, as a matter of fact," said Manuel inserting the key into the ignition and starting the engine, "my maternal grandmother said that the lovely young lady I should meet here at the vast, sprawling, intimidating, intellectually over-sophisticated but lushly lovely campus of the University of British Columbia would resist my advances, and that I should see in that a sign of her worth—and I can see now that I have come to know you, that *Abuela* was certainly right."

"Your maternal grandmother said that!" exclaimed Jane. "But how—?

"Ah! I do not wonder at your bewilderment, Jane darling," he said, putting the shift stick into drive and pulling away from the curb—or kerb to give it its hoity-toity British spelling. "As I mentioned, there is Gypsy blood in my veins coming as well from mother's side as from my father's, for my maternal great grandfather, instead of marrying, as the family had arranged and fully expected, the daughter of the Conde de Tarragona, fell in love with the Conde's darkly beautiful illegitimate daughter by a Gypsy sorceress and eloped with her—much to the disgust and annoyance of the family, of course."

"Oh—!" exclaimed Jane, somewhat shocked despite having come to expect the unexpected in Manuel's background.

"A terrible, scandal, of course, but my great grandfather, his father, my great great grandfather having recently died, was now the head of the family—as I am now of mine, my dear Padre having died a few years ago—"

"Oh, I'm so sorry, Manuel!" said Jane sympathetically touching his arm.

"*Gracias*," said Manuel, glancing at her with an appreciative smile. "I treasure your sympathy which is deeply touching. But to get on with my story, Great Grandpapa was head of the family and a man of high status and hereditary owner of vast estates, and so he was untouchable. There was nothing anyone could do about his scandalous marriage. They simply had to accept it. And to everyone's amazement, his gypsy sweetheart, my great grandmother, made him a fine and loyal wife, taking her place as mistress of his *casa* and hostess of his grand entertainments with such dignity and charm that soon the furor abated. Furthermore, his former betrothed married a vastly wealthy British industrialist who had been elevated to the peerage. So everything worked out well for all concerned."

"What a romantic story, Manuel!"

"Almost straight out of a Harlequin Romance."

"You are so full of surprises, Manuel!"

"I hope they do not trouble you, my darling Jane."

"No, although they do take some getting used to, but," she continued, to her own surprise at even entertaining the thought, much less expressing it, "they make you so much more wonderfully fascinating, darling."

"One does not have to have gypsy blood to be fascinating, dearest Jane. I know," he said with a twinkle in his eye, "a young lady from the free, open, clean and innocent Canadian Prairies who is the most remarkably fascinating woman I've ever met. And to be frank, having gypsy blood does not always engratiate one in the highest circles in Spain, for in the minds of many, Gypsies are the lowest of the low. But I certainly feel no shame. My great grandmother's gypsy blood has, without doubt, added new strength and vigor to mine."

"But your grandmother?" interposed Jane, still curious to know how that lady had known she would resist Manuel's advances. "Did she really tell you that you would meet me?"

"Not exactly, but before I left Spain to come here, she told my fortune with her Tarot cards and said that in Canada I would meet the woman for whom I had always been searching. She could not describe that woman but said I would know her as soon as I saw her, and that is exactly what happened when I saw you, Jane. I knew right away that you were the woman *Abuela* saw in the cards, the woman of my dreams. That partly explains my forwardness, my aggressiveness, for you see, I knew right away that you were meant to be mine."

Jane stared at him in amazement.

"Does that surprise you, Jane? Unsettle you perhaps?"

"In a way, yes, but not the way you may think. You see, my Grannie reads tea cups, and she read mine before I came out here to Vancouver— Poor old Grannie! She's such a dear, and I always feel I have to indulge her little whims—and she told me I would meet a tall dark man who would eventually win my heart. Oh—here's where I live."

Manuel pulled over to the curb, but when he had turned off the motor, they did not get out immediately. Manuel turned to her and said, "How utterly amazing! Tea leaves! Who would have believed it? Your British Grandmother could see in the tea leaves what my gypsy sorceress grandmother could see in the Tarot cards!"

"Actually, my Grannie is Scots—though born in Ireland."

"Ah! A Celt! No wonder!"

"Truly, Manuel, you—and Hamlet—are right: There are more things in heaven and earth than you can shake a stick at. No-no." said Jane wrinkling up her forehead. "That's not right. That follows not."

"Than all get out?" suggested Manuel, but immediately ecognized that he too was wrong. "That's not it either. However, that's the gist of what he said. But tell me, Jane, if your grandmother told you that you'd meet a tall, dark man, why did you resist me so long—apart from the fact that it was in the cards—and in the tea leaves—that you would?"

"I'm afraid I just never put much stock in that sort of thing, and besides, Grannie is so veddy, veddy British and doesn't believe that anything good can come from outside the British Isles that I simply couldn't imagine her envisaging a Spaniard. I—uh—I don't share her views, by the way," Jane added hurriedly.

"I am glad of that," said Manuel taking her into his strong, masculine arms and almost crushing her in his fiercely and ardently passionate, intensely urgent embrace, and bringing his hard, aristocratic mouth down like hot iron on Jane's soft, warm and now more than receptive lips so that she felt her blood turn to molten lava and her bones to limp, flaccid gelatin.

Oh Manuel! Do you intend to take advantage of this naive, helpless and all too loving young woman to destroy her innocence? And Jane, have you become too ready to lose your innocence? I really feel this is much too soon, that it should not happen until much later in the novel.

"Oh Jane! Jane! Jane!" breathed Manuel, sighing deeply.

"Oh Manuel! Manuel! Manuel!" suspired Jane.

"My darling!"

"My dearest!"

"My joy!"

"My treasure!"

"My heart!"

"My soul!"

"My life!"

"My light!"

"My all!"

"My beloved!"

"My one and only!"

"My ain true love!"

"Wh—? Your what?"

"Oh—It's Scots. My one true love."

"Oh, I see. Well, as I was about to say, my beautiful, sensitive, loving Jane!"

"My strong, handsome, darling Manuel!"

"Oh!"

"Oh!"

He drew her so close and so tightly to him that he almost crushed the breath out of her, and she felt her bones would crack—though she wondered how that could happen when they had already turned to flaccid gelatin.

"Oh Manuel! Please! Please! You're—you're hur—"

He released her but continued to gaze at her.

"Oh Jane, my darling! I have waited so long for this moment that I got carried away! I was becoming afraid you would never be mine, that I'd never hold you in my arms and call you my own. You are my own, are you not, dearest Jane?"

"Oh yes, Manuel! Completely, utterly, totally!"

"And I, dearest Jane, all unworthy though I be, am completely, utterly, totally yours!"

"Oh Manuel! It is I who am unworthy! That a nobody from the Canadian Prairies should be the choice of a Spanish aristocrat—"

"Oh Jane! There you go putting yourself down again! It is I who am unworthy of so beautiful and talented a young woman as you!"

"Oh no, Manuel! I—"

"Oh yes, Jane!"

"Would you like to come in for coffee?"

"Yes, Jane dearest, I would love to come in for coffee."

Manuel was too dignified and aristocratic to run to open the door on the passenger side and extend his hand to assist Jane to get out, but he did walk very briskly, and then they walked arm in arm to the door of her basement suite, like Alison's, over-priced and under-heated, but her port in the storm and her refuge when in disgrace with misfortune and men's eyes. Suddenly, Jane wondered at her own temerity bringing into this

Oh Jane, my lovely heroine! What are you thinking?

As these thoughts coursed through Jane's mind, they arrived at the door of her apartment, and there Manuel again took her into his arms and planted on her lovely and more than eager lips such a long, lingering, warm, intense, fervent, eager, yearning, sensuous, amorous, erotic and really very nice kiss that Jane lost all hesitation. And after all, Manuel was an Anglican, for he himself had said it, and it's greatly to his credit that he is an Anglican—well, a member of the Spanish Reformed Episcopal Church in communion with Anglicanism.

So thinking, she fumbled in her gold handbag for her key—after Manuel had released her from his embrace, of course—and opened the door to let him in.

Oh Jane! Oh Jane! Know'st thou what thou dost? Let's thou the wolf into thy fold, the lion to thy haven, the devil into thy sanctuary? Art thou about to betray my trust? Oh Jane! Greatly do I fear for thee! Desperately do I fear for thee! Oh Jane! Do be careful!

"I'm afraid it's not very luxurious," she said as they entered. "I've tried to make it comfortable, but I'm sure it's nothing like what you're accustomed to."

"It is yours, Jane," said Manuel, as, like the gentleman he was, he helped her out of her coat. "That is all that matters. And," he said glancing about him, "you have made it very comfortable and homelike—or as my English nanny Miss Geraldine Fitzhenry would say, homely."

Oh Manuel! Please do not find it too comfortable and homelike, I beg you! Remember that you have Jane, but a sweet, innocent fledgling only just out out of the parental nest, at your advantage, and that you are a *gentilhombre Espanol*! I beg you, do not try to help her out of more than her coat!

Manuel wandered about the aprtment survbeying the reproductions, the Chinese bamboo hangings, and the Wes Coast Canadian Indian prints which adorned her walls, the colorful rugs with which she had covered the cracked and broken linoleum on her floor, and the inexpensive but tasteful and comfortable pieces with which she had furnished the large room that made it seem much warmer and more pleasant than in fact it was.

Oh Manuel! Why does your eye linger so long on the bed? What nefarious thoughts infest your imagination?

"Why Jane!" exclaimed Manuel. "It is charming, utterly charming! Such exquisite taste! Such warmth! Such comfort! Such refinement! It is you, Jane!"

"Why, thank you Manuel," said Jane. "It's really very simple."

"Ah, but such exquisite simplicity!"

"Thank you again, Manuel, but do sit down while I make coffee. Perhaps you'd like to listen to some music? I have a CD of songs by Falla and Garcia Lorca song by Teresa Berganza."

"Ah!" he sighed as he seated himself on the couch. "Teresa Berganza!" A gleam of nostalgia filled his eyes. "A woman of charm, warmth, poise and consummate artistry!"

"Do you know her?" asked Jane in some astonishment as she took the CD from the rack.

"Know her? No, not really. I have met her on several occasions after recitals. The first time was when I was twelve and she a beautiful young woman—just the sort of woman for a young boy to idolize and to set his heart aflame. Padre took me backstage to meet her and she was very gracious, and naturally, as young twelve year old boys are wont to do in such circumstances, I fell in love with her and have remained so ever since."

"Oh!" exclaimed Jane and almost dropped the CD on the floor.

"Fear not, Jane, my love. One of those adolescent infatuations that never quite goes away."

"I—I suppose so," said Jane, somewhat reassured. "I guess I've felt a little bit that way about Robert Redford ever since I first saw him in a movie."

"Much the same thing I'm sure."

Now fully reassured, Jane inserted the CD into the player and the beautiful mezzo-soprano voice filled the room as she began to measure out the coffee into the cage and fill the coffee maker with water. Manuel sat on the couch, his head back, staring at the ceiling, and in that pose she found him when she placed a tray with cream, sugar and a plate of cookies on the coffee table in front of him. Again he seemed to her a soul in torment, and she wanted desperately—felt he desperately needed her—to calm his nerves, to reach out to him to ease his pain, to soothe his savage breast, to allay the tumult in his soul, to pour oil on the troubled waters of his spirit, his nerves, to be, in other words, the consoling, caring, compassionate woman heroines of romantic novels are supposed to be.

But be wary of such feelings, Jane, noble though they be! Too often have they led a sweet, innocent young woman in the first blush of love to self-betrayal.

"Do—do you enjoy the music, Manuel, my beloved?" she inquired hesitantly.

"Ah! *Si*! Yes! Yes indeed! It takes me back in thought at least to my home in Spain!"

"Then I hope the coffee will also do that, for it is Spanish roast."

"Ah Jane! You are most considerate! But everything you do and everything you is admirably fabulous and so fabulously admirable!"

"You always say the nicest things. Manuel," said Jane with her loveliest smile. "I'll get the coffee."

She returned with two cups of steaming, aromatic coffee, gave one to Manuel and with the other sat down close beside him on the couch.

Manuel sipped his coffee and said, "Ah Jane! That is delicious! You make excellent coffee! One could not find better in the bazaars of Barcelona and Madrid! It does indeed remind me of Spain!"

"You must miss your country," Jane said tenderly.

"I do, yes. Ah *Espana*! The agony and the ecstasy! The magnificence and the squalor! The passion and the ennui! The high civilization and the barbarity! Ah Spain! Spain!"

She had never seen him like this and moved even closer to him to place a reassuring hand upon his shoulder.

"You must love your country very dearly," she said.

"Every Spaniard loves his country with a passion and hates with an equal passion every other Spaniard who does not love it in the same way he does. We cheerfully kill one another crying out as we do *'Arriba Espana!'*"

"But surely now with the new King—"

"Ah, true, true! His Majesty has made a great difference and allayed many of the old hostilities. Ah Jane!" he sighed, his tone almost pleading.

He took a last sip of coffee, set down his cup, turned to her and reached out to take her in his arms. Again as his lips pressed down on hers, she felt her blood turn to molten lava and her bones to flaccid gelatin as she fell backward on the sofa with Manuel bending over her and pressing against her in his passionate embrace. She felt his hands stroking her thighs, her flanks, and her breasts as though what she once felt he was doing with his eyes he was now about to do with his hands, and she felt that if he did, she would not—

Jane! Jane! Do not yield so easily! And Manuel, I beg you, do not take advantage of a sweet girl in the first ardor of love!

Suddenly Manuel drew back, sat up, drew from his breast pocket a handkerchief of the finest French silk and mopped his fevered and perspiring brow.

"Wh—what is wrong, Manuel?"

"Oh Jane! What you do to me! The effect you have on me! It's frightening! I almost—! May I have another cup of coffee?"

"C—certainly, Manuel," said Jane standing up and straightening her dress. "I—I—You—Cream and sugar? I forget."

"No thanks, just black."

Quickly Jane ran to refill his cup, and he took a rather large gulp which must have burned his throat, but he made no protest.

"Thanks," he said. "Whew! Oh!"

"Manuel," said Jane, "don't be upset. It's all right. I mean—"

She again seated herself beside him and gently touched his arm. He took her hand in his and turned to her.

"Jane, I hope you realize that I hold you in the highest regard and have nothing but the deepest respect—that I will always honor—"

"Oh yes, Manuel! You—I—we—"

"You make superb coffee, Jane," he said, taking another mouthful.

Oh Manuel! I am proud of you! You have behaved like the true *gentil-hombre* I knew you to be. My faith in you is restored! I know now that I can trust sweet loving Jane to your care. But Jane! Jane! Be careful! Do not let the excitement in your blood take possession of you and lead you down the primrose path of dalliance like a puffed and reckless libertine!

—What a strange and complex man he is, thought Jane. I thought for a moment that he wanted to—to—t—take away my—that I was going to l—lo—lose my—that I would no longer be a v—vir—that he was going to violate my chaste treasure. But he drew back. He is such a man of such strange contradictions—such intense passion combined with such old fashioned honor! When I first knew him I thought he was—But then I thought that he—And now again tonight I again began to think he was—I hardly know what to think, except that I know I love him and that he loves me, so would it be a violation if he were—if I were—if we were—Oh dear! Is this really me thinking like this!

"Uh—it's getting late, Jane," said Manuel interrupting her musing, "so I suppose I should go."

"Oh—uh—yes," said Jane, glancing at her watch. "I had no idea it was getting so late. With thee conversing I forget all time. But you don't have to—"

"Ah Jane! This has been the most wonderful evening of my entire life! I wish neither to spoil the memory of it not to wear out my welcome. But on the last day of term, would you have dinner with me and let me take you dancing afterward?"

"Oh Manuel! That sounds lovely! I'd be delighted!"

"You have a formal evening gown?"

"Oh—uh—yes, I have a gown, but it's rather out of style." The fact is she had left it in Saskatoon, for the last time she had worn it she had been with—Donald!—and it brought back unpleasant memories. "But," she hurried to add, "I've a bit of money saved up and just today I received a letter—which CUPW managed to deliver in just under four weeks—with a generous gift from my parents—though they're not wealthy, yet they are not poor either, and can afford to keep me reasonably in style, so I can buy a new one."

"Wonderful! Perhaps I might accompany you as you make your selection?"

"Oh, yes—if you wish. You have such wonderful ideas about attire and fashion."

"Then I'll arrange things with you as the time draws near."

"Thank you, Manuel, darling! And oh! A formal evening! How romantic!"

She accompanied him to the door where he again took her into his arms for a long lingering kiss and an even longer and lingeringer embrace.

"Good night, Jane dearest!" said Manuel.

"Good night, Manuel, darling!" said Jane. "Good night. Good night. Parting is such sweet sorrow that I must say good night till it be morrow."

"Sleep dwell upon thine eyes, peace within thy breast," he said. "Would that I were sleep and peace so sweet to rest."

Jane stood at her door waving as she watched depart him who likewise waved and looked back at her, as with his head over his shoulder turned, he seemed to find his way without his eyes, for to his Lamborghini he went without their helps, and to the last bended their light on her.

Later, at about three o'clock in the morning, Jane awoke with a start and immediately ran to the phone to dial Manuel's number. To her surprise Manuel answered without the phone's ever ringing.

"Jane!" he exclaimed. "I'd just picked up my phone to dial you! I just awoke with a start remembering how that line from Hamlet should go!"

"Manuel! You did? So did I! It's 'There are more things in heaven and earth than are dreamt of in your philosophy, Horatio.'"

"Exactly what came to me! Jane! We are of one mind!"

"Oh yes, darling! Soul mates!"

"I've always known it!"

"And how right you were, darling!"

"I love to hear you call me 'darling', Jane dearest."

"Oh, and I love to call you 'dearest', Manuel darling. But I must let you return to your rest, but I just had to phone to tell you—darling."

"And I'm so glad you did, dearest. It is joy unbounded just to hear your voice no matter the time of day or night."

"And for me to hear yours, too, darling. I could listen to you all night long—except that it is now, strictly speaking, morning."

"Yes. Then fare thee well, my love, and fare thee well a while, and I will come to thee, my love, love though it were ten thousand mile. But of course, it's only as far as campus, and it's you who will be coming out here—Now why," he said, a thought seeming to strike him suddenly, "don't I come to pick you up in the Lamborghini?"

"That would be lovely, darling. But you must come for breakfast."

"That would be delightful, Jane, my dearest. See you about eight?"

"Yes. So bye until then, darling."

"Until then, my dearest."

—How much simpler, thought Jane as she replaced the receiver, if he had stayed the night. Oh dear! What am I thinking! But we are in love, after all, so why—? Oh dear me! Deary, deary me! What am I thinking! What is happening to me!

CHAPTER THE EIGHTH

For lovely young Jane Doe, returning for Christmas to her paents' home in Saskatoon—that middle-sized city with delusions of grandeur in the heart of the free, open, clean and innocent Canadian Prairies—had been to experience mixed feelings. She felt her whole being cleft in twain, cut into halves, split in two and carved down the middle. It had been wonderful, of course, to be with her loving, supportive and generous parents again and pleasant to visit old friends from school and undergraduate days, but she had left her heart on the West Coast in the sprawling, worldly-wise—and just plain worldly—slightly decadent and perhaps somewhat wicked but exciting and gorgeously situated city of Vancouver with Manuel Fernando de Ortega y Diaz de Rodriguez. It was, therefore, the best of times, it was the worst of times, a happy time, a sad time. And so, on one of those cold Prairie winter evenings, while Jane sat gazing at the lighted Christmas tree in her parents' simply furnished but cozy living room, her feet tucked beneath her on the sofa, many a sigh broke from her anxious breast.

"Are you in love with someone back there in Vancouver?" her mother had asked.

"Wh—? Oh, no thanks, Mother," she had replied absently. "Not right now."

Her mother looked at her, puzzled for a moment, and then smiled to herself, feeling she had her answer.

"Well, I hope he's very nice," said her mother.

"Oh yes, Mother, it has been lovely—as always."

But it was not just missing Manuel that distracted her thoughts. Her memories of their last night together, which should have been so happy, Manuel having treated her so wonderfully, were troubled and unsettled, and it was not just the strange, un-Jane Doe-like thoughts that had been going through her mind ever since her paper on Donne's *Songs and Sonets*, those exuberantly sensual lyrics which explored every aspect—spiritual, emotional and physical—of being in love and that had come disturbingly close to the surface when Manuel had taken her home after Alison's party. No, she was beginning to come to terms with those feelings and to know how she would behave when, in Veronica's wisdom, the time came for her to yield to them. It was something else, something deeply unsettling that had occurred on that last night before leaving Vancouver.

Manuel had entertained her for dinner in the luxurious penthouse he had rented atop Cornwall Manner in the University Endowment Lands. She had worn her new deep blue evening gown with a trim of white fur in which Manuel, who had accompanied her on her purchasing expedition, had said she looked gorgeous. Her initial embarrassment that in this gown her lovely, creamy-complexioned, smooth-as-silk shoulders were ex—exp—expo—were b—b—ba—were uncovered, soon vanished, and she felt completely at ease and happy as they dined on the sumptuous meal prepared by Manuel's own chef and served by his personal valet and with an excellent choice of wines, brandy and liqueurs. Ah! It has been the most romantic of evenings as they lingering over their coffee to the strains of Mozart played in the living room by Vancouver's famed Jeremiah Clarke String Quartet hired by Manuel for the occasion—a great improvement, Jane felt, over the usual accompaniment to her frugal but nourishing and tasty meals, the CBC program whose host, though his choice of music was generally good, other than the Bach playing of a certain Canadian pianist who seemed to believe that the Leipzig master wrote for the Well-tempered Anvil and for the songs of a pop singer who won awards for singing through her nose and of another who won awards for caterwauling like a cat, made such inane attempts at humor as to drive her almost to the point of smashing her portable radio against the wall. Long sat they thus, gazing out over the houses of University Hill Village brightly lit up for Advent, before departing to dance at the ballroom of the Hotel Vancouver—on one of the last occasions when that could happen, for soon afterwards the hotel decided to close the ballroom. Manuel helped her into the magnificent satin-lined evening cloak which he had bought for her as a Christmas present to wear over her gown, and they descended to the main entrance and walked to his bright red Lamborghini parked by the curb. As he held the door for her to enter, she thought she had seen lurking behind a tree a female figure with long dark hair combed over one eye, the figure of Yvette la Flambee!

Ever since the night of Alison's party, Yvette had been making her meretriciously glamorous presence felt and her amorous intentions toward Manuel obnoxiously obvious. On several occasions when Jane and Manuel had been enjoying an intimate tete-a-tete over coffee in Yum-Yum's cafeteria, Yvette, with a studied casualness had minced by in her twelve point seven centimetre heels, fluttering her obviously false eyelashes—Jane wondered if anything else about her physical appearance was false—toward Manuel and singing out in saccharine tones as she passed, "Buenos dias, Manuel Fernando de Ortega y Diaz de Rodriguez!" and pretending that Jane was not there. Several times, glancing out the window of the sixth-floor English Department Reading Room, Jane had seen la Flambee, arms waving, chasing after Manuel as he walked toward the Main Library, and Manuel, much to her relief, pretending not to hear her, until—Oh horrors!—she had managed to catch up with him in her twelve point seven centimetre stiletto heels—no mean feat, and, alas! proof of her determination. Another time from the same sixth floor window Jane had witnessed Yvette accosting Manuel as he emerged from C Block of the Buchanan Classroom Complex and engaging him in conversation, backing him with every mincing step she took closer and closer to the wall until she had imprsoned him in a corner of the building with her too too ample frontal endowment—could it really be that ample?—within centimetres of his chest. Again, to Jane's relief, Manuel managed to sidle out of his entrapment.

But now, for a week, she had left him alone in Vancouver exposed, and perhaps, without her presence, vulnerable, to the machinations of that vampire. Yvette was entirely capable, she felt, of arriving at the door of Manuel's penthouse in her stiletto heels and sable coat with nothing on underneath, and she shuddered to think of her unclad body reclining voluptuously on the plush maroon velvet sofa or stretched prone on a tiger skin before the fireplace—Jane could not remember there being a tiger skin before the fireplace, but she would not put it past Yvette to provide one—ankles crossed, elbows propped up on the tiger's head, chin resting on her folded hands, and her exposed green eye gazing lustfully and enticingly at Manuel. Would Manuel's old-fashioned sense of honor be strong enough to resist such temptation?

And now, on the morning of December 31, just as Jane was preparing to depart for the airport to fly to Vancouver to spend New Year's Eve with Manuel, the inevitable in this kind of fiction happened. A telegram addressed to her was delivered to her parents' door. With trembling hands Jane opened it and read:

SORRY CANNOT MEET YOU AT AIRPORT OR KEEP DATE AS PROMISED. CALLED AWAY TO SPAIN ON URGENT MATTER. MANUEL

Her heart skipped a beat. The bottom fell out of her life. Her dreams burst like a bubble. Her world collapsed like a house of cards. A dark cloud fell over her hopes. It rained in her soul. She felt really upset.

—Oh! she thought. I should never have let him out of my sight! Urgent matter indeed! That minx has got through to him! The cat! The vixen! The serpent! She worked her wiles on him and got her fangs into him! She went to his penthouse just as I feared and aroused his passions by presenting herself to him n—na—n—nu—uncl—without her clothes, and he's off with her on a wild, sensual, erotic orgy in Las Vegas or some such sinkhole of sin and depravity! And I'm sure there are such places in Spain if that is really where he has gone! Oh why did that minx have to come into my life just when I'd found my one true love? Why couldn't she have stayed in Siberia where she belongs—in a gulag! Oh—maybe they don't have gulags any more. Well, she could at least have stayed in Siberia, or married that Colonel of Militia in Moscow. Why did I not realize sooner how much Manuel meant to me so that I could have made him more securely mine? Why is my life so horrible? I'll enter a convent. Oh—I'm not a Roman Catholic. Well, there are Anglican religious orders, but they're a bit of an anomaly—rather like Presbyterian cathedrals. I wonder if women's liberation has reached the French Foreign Legion? Maybe I could join a circus or run off with the wraggle-taggle gypsies, oh. Oh, what shall I do? How can I go back to Vancouver and university now? Oh—I have my ticket and my fees are paid for the second term. I'll just have to absent myself from felicity a while and draw my breath in pain and face the music.

Then she thought, No! No! Jane Doe is no quitter! I'll show that minx what I'm made of! And I'll show that Judas what he has lost by throwing me over!

Thus resolved, Jane boarded her flight to Vancouver. Oh, her heart indeed was heavy, her spirits depressed, but her resolve was firm, and the first thing she did on her arrival was to go downtown to La Danieta Shoe salon and purchase a pair of bright red five-inch, or twelve point seven centimetre, stiletto heeled shoes with cross-over ankle straps—"*Signorina* will find they make it much easier to walk," the clerk had said—and then gone next door to Luxurious Leather to purchase a matching bright red leather mini-skirt.

—Two can play the game as well as one! she reflected resolutely. Yet for all her resolve Jane could not dispel her gloom as she sat alone on New Year's Eve in her over-priced, under-heated basement room thinking of the joy that might have been hers but was now Yvette la Flambee's who was probably wrapped around Manuel in a Las Vegas hotel suite or pressed against him in a skimpy see-through dress on the dance floor of some salacious dive in Tijuana. Do they have salacious dives in Tijuana? Jane hardly knew, but it did not really matter where they were. What mattered was that her man was with the Panther who had stolen him from her, that Manuel had betrayed her, had been unfaithful to her, had run off as his uncle had done with Miss Geraldine Fitzhenry, had left her for a cheap, disgusting trollop! And the next day, New Year's Day, when she had planned to cook a wonderful dinner for him, Jane sat alone sobbing to herself as she spooned into her mouth the cold contents of a can of pork and beans.

Jane was really in a bad way.

Yet when a day later it was time to return to campus, Jane resolved again to put a good face on everything and dressed herself in her new five-inch stilettos and her mini-skirt. And who should be the first person she saw on the opposite side of the East Mall as she stepped from the number 49 bus at the campus terminal? Who but Yvette la Flambee mincing along in her five inch stilettos, her frontal endowment wobbling up and down.

—What! The minx is still here! Perhaps he did not run off with her after all!

But where was he? Where did he go? That was the question. And why had he given no explanation? One would have thought he could at least have done that, surely. Would it not have been nobler in the mind to have done so? Perhaps there was a woman back in Spain. Had his family called him back insisting that her marry her? But no, he had told her he was the head of his family and could do as he wished. So why the mystery? Why was he keeping her in suspense like this? Oh, men could could be so thoughtless and cruel!

However, at least Jane felt reasonably confident that she knew who he wasn't with—with whom he wasn't—was not.

Deliberately, provocatively, Jane crossed the Mall and caught up with Yvette la Flambee.

"Did you have a pleasant holiday, Mademoiselle la Flambee?" asked Jane with affected sweetness.

"Oh, it's you," retorted Yvette contemptuously. "Well, it might have been better, but there was at least one bright spot."

Jane did not like the sound of that, but she was prevented from trying to discover what that bright spot might have been by Yvette's noting her attire and commenting thereon.

"Well! I see you have bought yourself a pair of twelve point seven centimetre stiletto heels and a miniskirt. Do you really think you can rival me? But I notice your shoes have ankle straps. Afraid you can't stay up in them without support?"

"Well," retorted Jane, not to be put down easily, "at least I can walk in mine instead of mincing along in little baby steps the way you do!"

"Oh!" flared Yvette la Flambee, too overwhelmed to be able to reply, but with her visible green eye narrowed and shooting out arrows of hatred.

Then, as though to prove that she could walk rather than mince, Jane gave a brief "Fare thee well!" and stepped out with a firm gait leaving la Flambee far behind in the dust. Actually, she left her behind in the spray and the mist, for, as it frequently does at that time of year in Vancouver, it had begun to drizzle.

Later that day over coffee with April, May, June, Julia, Augusta and Catherine, Jane received information that, if not exactly encouraging, was not completely discouraging.

"We haven't seen Manuel Fernando de Ortega y Diaz de Rodriguez around campus for the last few days," said Julia, "Do you know where he is, Jane?"

Jane blushed.

"Well," she said, "he—uh—he left me a m—message that he'd be out of town for a few days—gone back to Spain on some urgent business—b—but he didn't say what."

"I must say, Jane," said April, "we're glad that at least you heard from him. We were afraid for a while that it might have been something else. The Panther—la Flambee, you know—has certainly been stalking him and laying wait for him, and we were afraid that—well—that, you know, she'd, like, got through to him and, maybe, persuaded him, you know, to take her away somewhere."

"Oh—!" gasped Jane, her old fears resurfacing.

"She was all over him at Maxine Maxwell's party," said May.

"Absolutely disgusting!" exclaimed June, throwing up her hands in horror.

"But," said Catherine, placing her hand reassuringly on Jane's, "Manuel resisted her blandishments with admirable fortitude. I don't know where he gets such strength. La Flambee usually gets her way with men—especially other women's men."

"Yes," said Augusta, "it was utterly attrocious the way she took Clarence Avenue away from Heather Street, and then dumped him after she'd had her use of him—if you get what I mean. That's her way. But it seems she's met her match in Manuel. Strange, because I originally thought he represented the same thing in a male."

"We all did," said April, "but he's been standing up with unexpectedly manful fortitude, but it must be taking an awful toll on him."

"Yes," said Augusta. "He was drinking profusely at Maxine's party as though he needed the fortification of alcohol to resist la Flambee's wiles, but the amazing thing was that all that liquor didn't seem to affect him. Anyone else would have passed out on the floor if he'd taken in as much as he did. He must have a very strong head for liquor, but I hate to think of the terrific hangover he must have wakened to the nest morning."

—Just as long as he didn't waken to Yvette la Flambee! thought Jane.

"Yvette stayed behind seething with rage when he left," said May, "but I don't know how long he can stand up to her. She's very persistent."

Again Jane felt her heart sink, the rain descend in her soul, the dark clouds descend on her future and her whole world collapse about her like a house of cards.

"So we were glad," said Julia, "to see la Flambee on campus this morning. At least it suggests that she's not with him."

"I hope this is not upsetting you, Jane," said April, "for we think he rather likes you, and it seemed at Alison's party that you rather like him, so we thought you should have fair warning."

"Yes," said June. "Hold onto him tight because the Panther is out to get him."

June's words put fibre into Jane's soul, iron into her sinews, fire into her blood, determination into her mind and strength into her heart. If la Flambee wished to sow the whirlwind, she would reap the whirlwind! Jane would fight for her man! She would not yield to the enemy! She would not give up the ship or yield an easy victory to the foe! If she went down, she would go down fighting! She would fight in the Reading Room! She would fight in the library! She would fight at parties! She would fight in Yum-Yum's Cafeteria!* She would not flag nor fail! She would go right on to the end! She would never surrender!

"Those red five-inch spikes and the miniskirt should certainly help," said Catherine.

"Yes indeed!" said April. "In those heels you tower above la Flambee!"

"And you look ten times better in them," said April. "You've got much nicer legs."

"Your breasts aren't as big, but they're okay," said Augusta.

"In fact, much better proportioned," said June. "Hers are really rather grotesque. Quite frankly, I'd be happy if mine were as nice as yours, Jane."

"Oh!" said Jane, embarrassed. "Gee! Thanks!"

Her friend's comments suggested that perhaps her strategy was the right one, and imperiling her clothing budget for the next couple of months, she went downtown that very evening and bought another pair of twelve point seven centimetre stiletto heels and another leather miniskirt.

Black.

Which she wore the next day.

And the next.

Thus she would fight the Panther on her own turf.

CHAPTER THE NINTH

It was the third day of her return to campus and Jane had still not heard from Manuel. Such neglect, she felt, was both remiss and callous. To try to keep her mind off her keen disappointment and to relieve her heart of its sadness and the ache in her soul, she doggedly pursued her studies. And thus it was that as she sat in the Reading Room forcing herself to compare the Craig-Bevington text of *Hamlet* with that in the *Norton Facsimile edition of the First Folio* for a bibliography assignment, a shadow fell across the pages. Remembering that in Chapter the Third when a shadow had fallen across the page of *The Faerie Queene* it had been cast by Manuel Fernando de Ortega y Diaz de Rodriguez, she looked up eagerly and hopefully. But her eagerness quickly turned to shock and her hope to horror when she stared into the face of him who, in fact, had cast the shadow, a face from her past, a past that she thought was past, over and done with, gone forever. What turn of outrageous fortune's wheel had brought it back?

"Donald!" she exclaimed as she recognized her erstwhile would-be lover and s—se—sedu—her would-be ra—ra—rav—her would-be d—de—debau—the guy who would have undone her if she had let him, a faint but hopeful smile on his lips, a yearning, soulful glow in his eyes.

"Jane!" he whispered piteously. "They told me I might find you here. But Jane, you've changed. I hardly recognized you. You've let your golden locks fall to your shoulders in long, voluptuous tresses as I always wanted you to but you never would do it for me," he said wistfully, regretfully, sadly.

Recovering her composure and her late resolution to stand up for herself and not be pushed around like a plaything of fate, Jane replied in a cool, level voice, or as the French say, *avec sang froid*, "I wear my hair as I please to wear it, Donald. But what, may I ask, brings you out here to the sprawling and intimidating, intellectually over-sophisticated but lushly lovely campus of the University of British Columbia in worldly-wise and perhaps just plain worldly, somewhat decadent and perhaps slightly wicked but exciting and gorgeously situated West Coast city of Vancouver?"

Donald fell to his knees before her, his hands clasped together as though in prayer—probably for the first time in his life and to the wrong deity—even though Jane did have the beauty and the stature of a Greek goddess.

"You, Jane! You!" he cried, grasping her hand and covering it with kisses. "I cannot live without you!"

"Yech!" exclaimed Jane quite audibly this time as with her aforementioned *sang froid* she yanked her hand from his grasp and gave it a shake as though to rid herself of contamination. "I am afraid, Donald, that you will just have to manage to do so, for I can live quite easily without you. It is over between us."

"Oh, Jane, my beloved! Must you be so cruel! I have changed, my darling. I am not the man I was."

"I should certainly hope you're not," responded Jane. "You acted like an animal, Donald."

"Oh, how can such harsh and cruel words proceed from such lovely lips? Yet they are but just. I did act like an animal, Jane. I do confess it."

"You used me, Donald, as though I were an object to be possessed and manipulated."

"Oh Jane! I used you as though you were an object to be possessed and manipulated."

"Your conduct was utterly disgusting."

"Oh Jane! I realize now that my conduct was utterly disgusting."

"Your behavior was inexcusable and unforgivable."

"My behavior was inexcusable and unforgivable."

"So you cannot blame me if I hate even the memory of you, Donald, that I obscenity in the milk of your memory."

"Oh Jane! I cannot blame you if you hate even the memory of me, if perhaps even you were to obscenity in the milk of my memory."

"Is there an echo in this room?" she asked, looking about her.

"Is there as an an echo—Wha—? Oh—yes—uh—! But Jane, my dearest!" he implored. "Search in your heart to find some pity for a wayward soul. I have seen the error of my ways. I have changed, Jane. I am a new person. Please, Jane! Oh please, my dear one, my angel, *cara mia, mein liebchen, ma petite choux*, take me back, oh please take me back!"

"Oh Donald! Get up off your knees and stop kissing the toe of of my five-inch or twelve point seven centimetre stiletto-heeled shoe. Your abject simpering can no more win me than your former amorous lechery, nor am I impressed with your linguistic facility—which you probably acquired from a dictionary of foreign expressions. You can plead till the cows come home, till all the seas run dry and the rocks melt in the sun, I will not take you back! Never! Never! Never! Not in a thousand years! Not in a million years! Not if you were the last man on earth! Not if you were as rich as Rockefeller! Not if you were the King of England! Not if you were the Aga Khan! Not even if you were the Akound of Swat!"

"Oh Jane! Is there someone else?"

—Oh why, Jane agonized inwardly, did he have to ask that at this time?

Boldly, however, she answered him, "There just might be, Donald. There just might be."

Donald staggered to his feet, smashed his hand to his forehead and collapsed against the section of bookshelf containing PS3511 A86 Z866 to PS3562 O97 G7 in the Library of Congress classification system and cried, "Oh this is intolerable! How can I live without my life! How can I live without my soul!"

"Oh Donald! Don't be so Byronic!"

"It's not Byron, it's Emily Bronte."

"I know that, but Heathcliff is a Byronic figure, his literary forebear being Byron's Manfred."

"Oh there you go again!" cried Donald. "Always showing that you know more than I! If I got a B+, you got an A-; if I got and A-, you got a straight A. If I struggled and strove and swatted and burned the midnight oil at both ends to get an A, you got an A+!"

"So that's it! Now I know why you wanted to—to—to do what you wanted to do on that last night! It was jealousy! It was an inferiority complex! You wanted to show that you could dominate me! But Donald, I was never trying to one-up you, only to be the best scholar I could be. Surely that's the whole point of going into the graduate program. Well! Now I know you!"

Donald crumpled to the floor in a heap and began to snivel.

"Oh Jane! I confess it! You always seemed so much smarter than I, your scholarship so much more brilliant! I felt I was a nobody beside you!"

The multitude of scholars who habitually thronged the Reading Room in pursuit of greater erudition had been looking on this scene in utter amazement until Alison, the Reading Room attendant, at last took a hand and spoke reprovingly.

"Jane, I must request politely that you and your friend cease conducting yourselves in this manner or else depart from the Reading Room."

"Yes, Donald," said Jane, "we're disturbing everyone. At least if you'll promise, you miserable wretch, to control yourself and stay away from the subject we've just been discussing, I'll let by-gones be by-gones so far as to buy you a coffee."

"Oh would you do that for me, Jane?" sniveled Donald, again clasping his hands together in abject gratitude. "Oh, I hardly deserve such favor!"

"No you do not, but never let it be said that Jane Doe cannot be gracious now and then. Come on, wretch. Get up. Stand on your feet like a man!"

Donald wrenched himself to his feet as Jane rose from her chair. He stared at her and gasped.

"Jane! In five-inch or twelve point seven centimetre heels you—you tower over me! You never used to wear heels like those!"

"That I now realize, you pathetic worm, was because you could not bear to have me stand taller than you. Well, five-inch stiletto heels are very much in fashion now, and I'll wear them if I want to wear them. Now come along, you miserable excuse for a human being. Let's go for coffee."

How right Manuel had been, she reflected, to encourage her to dress fashionably and to find selfconfidence through her attire, to clothe herself in self-awareness, self-possession, self-motivation and self-propulsion. Now was she more determined than ever not to lose the man she loved. Yes, she would stand tall, hold her head erect and stare adversity full in the face, knowing that she, Jane Margaret Doe from the free, open, clean and innocent Canadian Prairies, could meet affliction head on and emerge from the fray, her head bloody, perhaps, but unbowed. She was a new and worldly-wise and just plain worldly, slightly decadent and somewhat wicked Vancouver had better watch out! Excelsior! Damn the torpedoes! Full speed ahead! Charge! *La garde ne se rend jamais*! Remember the Alamo! *Ils ne passerent pas*! Don't give up the ship! *Alt for Norge*! Go for broke! *Tenno haika banzai!* God for Harry! England and Saint George! *Per ardua ad astra!* Up and at 'em! *Vive la Canadienne*!

With stately bearing and dogged tread, Jane marched from the Reading Room, Donald like a lovesick puppy fawning obediently at her heels—all twelve point seven centimetres of them.

*   *   *   *

Next day when she entered the Reading Room, her heart skipped a beat, for there was Manuel seated at his usual carrel poring over the 1997 volume of *Milton Studies*!

He's back! she gasped inwardly with delight. But then a dark reflection crossed her mind. Why didn't he call me? Why did he not try to get in touch? But a slight glimmer of hope penetrated her gloom. Perhaps he has only just arrived back this morning and has come here straight from the airport especially to meet me.

She started toward him, and Manuel looked up briefly, seemed to take in at a glance and with some astonishment her new look in mini-skirt and five-inch heels—her red ones today—but then to her dismay and chagrin, he turned again to his book, causing her to stop dead in her progress. But then, summoning up the new Jane Doe, she returned to her purpose and walked past his carrel.

"Hello, Manuel," she said, quietly, shyly, sweetly, remembering some of the winning qualities of the old Jane Doe.

To her utter discomfiture, Manuel looked up for but the briefest of moments, grunted an acknowledgement with an ever so slight nod and returned once more to his book. In that very instant, Jane saw Yvette la Flambee, a facsimile of the "Trinity Manuscript" of Milton's early poems open before her, seated in the carrel immediately behind him. A wickedly triumphant smile played over her immaculately glossed lips and a glint of fiendish delight flashed in her cat-like green eye—the one not masked by her seductively arranged panther-black locks. Jane's heart sank. So the

Panther had caught her prey, and the perfidious Spaniard had betrayed her after all! Inwardly quivering with disappointment and chagrin, seething with anger and jealousy in keeping with the requirements of this stage of a romance novel, she sought consolation in the pages of W. W. Greg's *Bibliography of the English Printed Drama to the Restoration*.

As Jane sat studying in her carrel, young Donald, his jacket all unbraced, no hat upon his head, his stockings fouled, ungartered and down-gived to his ankle, pale as his shirt (if only his shirt had been white and not pucey pink) his knees knocking each other, and with a look so piteous in purport as if he had been loosed out of hell to speak of horrors, comes into the Reading Room. He took Jane by the wrist and held her hard and fell to such perusal of her face as he would draw it. Long stayed he so until at last he raised a sigh so piteous and profound that it did seem to shatter all his bulk.

"Donald!" exclaimed Jane who had been looking at him in utter amazement. "What mean you by this show?"

"Jane! Jane!" he sobbed. "My heart! My soul! My life! I am in torment! I cannot live without you, Jane! Day and night under the hide of me there's an oh! such a hungry yearning burning inside of me! In the roaring traffic's boom, in the silence of my lonely room, I think of you, night and day, Jane!"

"Oh for heaven's sake, Donald!" said Jane rising from her carrel. "Stop being so melodramatic!"

But before Jane could say another word or Donald make response, Manuel had risen from his carrel, flung himself over to them, roared in high dudgeon, "So it is for this that you have thrown me over!" and flung himself from the Reading Room, flung himself down the stairs, flung himself out of the Buchanan Tower, flung himself into his Lamborghini and drove off in all directions.

"Manuel!" cried Jane as he stalked from the room. "I can explain!"

She made to follow after him, but Donald clung to her, trying with all his might to hold her back.

"Oh Jane!" he cried. "Jane, my darling!"

Jane yanked her hand from his grasp and landed a resounding slap across his cheek, sending him crashing into the book shelves and knocking *The Complete Works of Shelley* to the floor.

"See what you've done, Donald, with your fawning and sniveling! Get out of my life!"

Her whole being a-quiver with anger and desperation, she stepped over him and strode to the door.

"Jane!" cried Donald, picking himself up off the floor and fumbling about trying to restore *The Complete Works of Shelley* to the shelf in their proper order, "Does this mean we're through?"

"Never again darken my sight!" shouted Jane, turning to him in rage. "I never want to see you again as long as I live!"

"Quiet please in the library!" quoth Alison ever more in a loud stage whisper.

Jane turned and glared at her.

"Never shake thy gory locks at me," protested Alison. "All I did was tell Manuel when he came looking for you yesterday that you had gone to have coffee with an old flame."

"You what!" exclaimed Jane.

"All I did was tell Manuel when he came looking—"

"I know what you told him! So that's it! Alison, if you could have thought of something more stupid and damaging to say, you would have!"

"I thought all for the best," apologized Alison.

"Aha!" crowed Yvette la Flambee, rubbing her hands with glee. "He's mine! Manuel is mine!"

"Over my dead body!" retorted Jane, her anger reaching white heat.

"Any way you like, deary," cackled Yvette with a fiendish smirk.

"Don't count on it, you little viper! The dead body might be yours! You're dealing with the new Jane Doe!"

"Gee, she's beautiful when she's angry!" said young, handsome, Percy Byron Browning, who had wandered into these pages from a novel by another writer, looking up from his copy of Tennyson and from his bevy of admiring female undergraduate followers.

Meanwhile, with Yvette's high-pitched, witchlike cackle echoing in her ears, Jane had turned on her twelve point seven centimetre stiletto heels and hurried from the Reading Room in the hope of overtaking Manuel. She rushed down the three flights of stairs—no mean feat in twelve point seven centimetre heels—to the third floor Department Office but did not find him there, and no one reported having seen him. She rushed down to the ground floor and out of the Buchanan Tower, looked about her in all directions, but could see no sign of him. She went to the Main Library and systematically searched among the stacks to see if he were there, but he was not. Resignedly, knowing that in her state of mind any further attempt at study would be futile, she left the campus and returned to her basement apartment to drown her sorrow in a pot of herbal tea.

That evening she phoned Manuel's penthouse, but Miguel the valet informed her that the master had not returned.

Oh! Where was he? In his desperation, all the result of a horrible misunderstanding, had he sought out Yvette la Flambee, and were they at this very moment—Her imagination conjuring up a scene of steamy passion and unspeakably fleshly sensuality and lust, she threw herself, sobbing inconsolably, onto the bed.

CHAPTER THE TENTH

The following morning Jane arrived at the Reading Room to see Manuel sitting at a carrel in a far corner concentrating assiduously on *Milton Studies (1987)*. His face a mask of anguish, he glanced up at her briefly but said nothing. To her horror she saw Yvette la Flambee seated at a table nearby so that Manuel could not help seeing her whenever he might look up, and bent over the "Trinity Manuscript" so as to position strategically for his delectation her deep decolletage and breathing deeply to cause her more than ample breasts to rise and fall—also for Manuel's delectation. Jane seated herself at the maximum possible distance from them commensurate with being able to note their actions from the corner of her eye.

She was surprised suddenly to hear a male voice at her left elbow.

"Hello Jane!"

She looked up to see young, handsome PhD candidate Percy Byron Browning who was writing his dissertation on Tennyson's use of verbs in *The Idyls of the King*. In a novel by the young, beautiful and prodigiously talented Indo-Canadian writer Inderjit Kaur Chundar-Mukergee who had won the prestigious Emond Prize for Literature over a large and distinguished field of candidates including not only the distinguished Polish-Canadian writer Jan Marriottewski but even Veronica Verity, Jane had met Percy at a wild, harum-scarum party unparalleled in anyone's experience for tastelessness, indecorum and total lack of refinement and dignity; and despite the brilliance of the writing and her recognition that a novelist has the right, nay the duty, to record life as it really is in all its raw and hoary detail, she nevertheless hoped fervently that no writer would ever place her again in such horrendous circumstances, her perils in this present novel being quite bad enough, and so far as she could see at the moment, boding fair to become even worse. Percy Byron Browning, however, was completely innocuous—a nice fellow, of whom, when one had said that about him, one had said all there was to say. Still, he was undoubtedly handsome, and that, along with his apparently inexhaustible wealth—his father being President of the Sans Souci Brassiere Company in Toronto—was the probable reason for his having attracted such a large following of young female undergraduates.

"Oh, hello, Percy," said Jane noncommittally.

"You are looking absolutely lovely today."

"Oh—well, thank you, but I don't think I look any different today from the way I did yesterday."

"Ah yes. Well, yesterday your shoes and skirt were red, to day they're black, but you always look particularly lovely."

"Oh—well, thank you again."

—What, she wondered, is this leading up to? And how is Manuel taking all this?

She stole a glance in his direction to see his brow furrowed, his face dark. In the next moment she learned what Percy was leading up to.

"What I wanted to ask, Jane, was whether I might take you to dinner FridayEvening?"

"Oh—! Dinner—? Friday—? With you—?"

The invitation to dinner, despite her sense that Percy had indeed been leading up to something, nevertheless took her by surprise. She had thought he might have wanted to take her for coffee, perhaps, but not dinner. Again she glanced across at Manuel and noted that he was quite visibly agitated. Again Jane reflected on the fact that Manuel had never since his return tried to be in touch with her or since the previous day tried to discover the truth about her relationship with Donald.

—Why hasn't he spoken? And why do I always find him in such proximity to Yvette? Well, it would serve him right if I accepted Percy's invitation!

"Perhaps," said Percy, sounding a bit crestfallen, puzzled, no doubt, by Jane's delay in answering him while she meditated on her own situation with regard to Manuel, "you would like a little more time to think it over?"

"Why no, Percy," she said with a sweet smile. "I have thought it over. I'd be pleased to have dinner with you, Thank you for asking."

Were those Manuel's books that fell to the floor with such a loud clatter? Jane decided not to look. She did turn, however, and her heart sank when she heard Yvette la Flambee whispering, "It's all right, Manuel. I'm here!"

—Have I, wondered Jane apprehensively, made the wrong move? Have I acted too impulsively, too precipitately, too much out of pique?.

She felt some gratification, however, when she heard Manuel respond to Yvette, "Oh for heaven's sake! Don't bother me now!"

A few moments later he rose from his carrel and stalked out of the Reading Room.

Jane, her mouth agape, her eyes wide, looked after him.

"Is there something wrong, Jane?" asked Percy Byron Browning.

"Oh—uh—no—no, nothing—not really."

"Good. Then I'll see you Friday evening. Around seven?"

"Uh—yes—fine. I'll be ready. Uh—thanks, Percy."

The evening with Percy Byron Browning had been, as Jane had expected, notable for its vacuity, even though, over dessert and liqueurs, Percy had tried to turn the conversation to serious matters.

"You know, Jane," he began, "I think you and I have much in common."

"Oh? Like what, Percy?"

"Well, like literature, for one thing."

"Yes, but I'm a Renaissance specialist, and you're a Victorian."

"Oh, but what's a few centuries between people of like mind? But I was really thinking of something else. I cannot express it, but surely you and everyone have the notion that there is, or should be, an existence of yours beyond you. What were the use of creation if I were entirely contained here?"

"No, Percy, I'm afraid I've never had such a notion nor known anyone else who had. I think you have Emily Bronte too much on your mind, and as a number of critics have stated, the idea is almost incestuous. Even people most well matched, are not completely alike. Perhaps you read yourself too much into the literature you study, Percy. It's an easy habit to fall into. Remember, literature, though it mirrors life, is not life; it enables us, as Wendey Steiner says, to entertain an idea without seeing as a call to action. I think she has put the case very well."

"Oh—well—uh—I—maybe—uh—yes—uh—" stammered Percy, obviously disappointed. "You—you've never had such a notion?"

"No, Percy."

"No?"

"No."

"Oh—uh—well—um—What are your thoughts on synecdoche?"

"Nothing original beyond what can be found in a handbook of literary terms."

"Oh—well—uh—would you like some more coffee or another liqueur?"

"No, thank you, Percy," she said with her wonted sweet, but not encouraging, smile. "I think I've had enough. It has been a pleasant evening."

"Oh—uh—gee!" exclaimed Percy, flustered. "Do you have to leave now? I was just getting—"

But Jane had stood up from the table.

"Yes, I really think I should go, Percy. Thank you for dinner."

"Oh—well—I—yes—um—my pleasure."

CHAPTER THE ELEVENTH

The Monday following her date with Percy Byron Browning, Jane, having that morning taken in a set of in-class essays from her first year English class, avoided the Reading Room and ensconced herself in her window-less office in the Auditorium Annex to mark them, but again, after the first five depressing essays on the role of the narrator in *The Great Gatsby*, she found she had to flee to Yum-Yum's cafeteria to seek solace in caffeine. As she sipped her Mocha Java—she felt a change from Amoretto Almond would do her good—a shadow fell across the table, and she looked up, expecting she knew not whom, and to her great surprise, she found that once again the shadow had been cast by Manuel Fernando de Ortega y Diaz de Rodriguez.

"M—Manuel!" she stammered.

"*Buenos dias,* Jane," he said, his voice quivering with suppressed emotion. "May I sit down?"

"Certainly, *Senor* Ortega y Diaz de Rodriguez," said Jane, recovering her composure and her sang froid. "It's a free country, after all."

"'*Senor* Ortega y Diaz de Rodriguez'?" he said, reproachfully. "What happened to 'Manuel'?"

"Oh, well, Manuel, if you so prefer," she responded coolly. "Do sit down—Manuel."

Manuel seated himself, but for a moment did not speak, uncertain, it seemed, how to begin whatever it was he wanted to say. Jane, despite her external coolness, was inwardly in turmoil. Was this to be the moment of reconciliation? Or was it to be "Good-bye for ever"?

To break the ice, she said, "We certainly have been having some fine weather lately, haven't we?"

"I did not come here to discuss the weather, Miss Doe."

'Miss Doe'! This was the most unkindest cut of all, but then, perhaps she had asked for it.

"Then what, pray tell, have you come to discuss, *Senor* Ortega y Diaz de Rodriguez?"

"Jane? Why are you so cold and formal?"

"Do you find me cold and formal, Manuel? Do you not think I have reason to be?"

"Yes—at least it probably seems that way to you. That is why I have come to speak to you. I want to explain my recent behavior which must indeed have seemed very strange to you."

"Strange, Manuel?" she said, outwardly cool, calm, and collected. "Yes, I suppose one might call it strange. That is a way of putting it. 'Strange' is perhaps as good a word as any."

"Well, first, about the other day—last week—in the Reading Room. Alison finally got around to explaining everything to me about that fellow—Donald, I think is his name—"

"Oh—yes—Donald. A part of my past, a part I had dismissed completely and never expected it to materialize again, and I have now once again dismissed it completely."

"Yes, but when Alison said you had gone to have coffee with a former conflagration—"

"That's 'old flame'."

"Old flame—ah yes!—well, anyway, I became jealous. I thought an old love had been rekindled and you had deserted me. What else was I to think?"

"Oh—well—I—yes," said Jane, now feeling a bit sheepish, "I—I guess that was open to misunderstanding. I had to get him out of the Reading Room because he was causing such a disturbance."

"So I hear, and then he made another one the following day, and I'm afraid I overreacted—but I did not have the explanation at the time."

"I'm afraid," said Jane, looking down in embarrassment, "I lost control of myself too after you had left."

"Yes, I hear there were a lot of pyrotechnics—er—no—no, don't tell me—fireworks."

"I was so terribly angry because—because you misunderstood."

"Well, anyway, that part is cleared up—I hope."

"Except for Yvette la Flambee!" protested Jane, looking up again, her anger and hurt again surfacing.

"Yvette la Flambee?" he flared. "What about Yvette la Flambee?"

"You know right well, what I mean, Manuel Fernando de Ortega y Diaz de Rodriguez! She's always hanging about you!"

"Oh—yes," he responded testily. "Clings to me like a leech, and as with leeches, I have no desire to have her stuck to me, but, also like leeches, she's hard to shake off. It is certainly not by my invitation that she's always hanging about me."

"Oh—oh—I—I thought maybe—"

"Jane! Surely you have more faith in me than to think that!"

"Oh Manuel!" The emotional tension of the past week had become more than she could bear, and she burst into tears. "Oh Manuel! I'm just a poor, silly, weak, helpless, heart-sick girl who's terribly, terribly in love with you!"

Manuel reached across the table and placed his hand on hers.

"Jane, my love, my heart, my soul, my joy, my treasure!" he said simply, quietly, tenderly, affectionately, compassionately, consolingly, lovingly, endearingly, reassuringly, supportively and really very nicely. "I'm so relieved to hear you say that! But come, dry away your tears. All is well again. But I do want to explain my absence."

"Yes," said Jane, looking up and smiling through her tears. "I'm sure now that you can do so fully, completely and satisfactorily, but I was deeply hurt that you did not do so at the time."

"I'm sure you were, Jane, as I was afraid you would be, and I'm deeply sorry, but I had no time to explain. In the middle of the night before I was supposed to meet you, I received a phone call from the Spanish Foreign Minister demanding I come right away to Madrid. There was a flight leaving in an hour and he had booked me a seat on it, so I had to pack a bag and leave in a hurry."

"You had to go to Madrid? Why, Manuel?"

"Well, my great uncle Pedro Federico de Ortega y Diaz de Rodriguez de Sanchez y Martinez y Navasquez is el Duque de Pontevedra y Alicante—

"Oh—!" exclaimed Jane.

"Yes. He was involved in an incident in Gibraltar which incensed the British authorities and nearly resulted in an international contretemps. Since I am his nearest of kin, I had to go over there and try to help straighten matters out."

"You're his nearest of kin? Then you could become—"

"Possibly. Despite three marriages, Tio is childless—at least he has no children to speak of, and he has never acknowledged those, but to give the old reprobate credit where credit is due, he has supported them, though anonymously—and he is also brotherless and sisterless and therefore nephewless and nieceless—except for a grand nephew through his father's brother—me. However, he has recently taken up with a flamenco dancer whom he says he wants to marry. She, in fact, was the cause of the diplomatic incident."

"Oh?"

"Yes. As I'm sure you know, the sovereignty of Gibraltar is disputed. The British captured it from us in 1704—stole it from us, most Spaniards would say—and Spain has always wanted it back. The incident was connected with that issue. You see, this young woman—"

"The flamenco dancer?"

"Yes. She was engaged to dance at a night club in Gibraltar, and *Tio* went with her. She came out on stage wrapped in a Spanish flag, spread a Union Jack on the floor and proceeded to dance on it."

"Oh dear!"

"'Oh dear!' indeed! But that was only the beginning. As her dance drew toward its climax, she whipped off the Spanish flag, under which, of course, she was completely nude—"

"Oh—!" exclaimed Jane, shocked.

"—and, all the time waving the Spanish flag, continued dancing on the Union Jack on which, at the conclusion of the dance, she wiped her feet. Naturally, the British authorities were enraged, and demanded the Spanish government take action, and of course, in the circumstances they had to, even though secretly they approved the point of the demonstration—an assertion of Spanish sovereignty—but took the position that the young woman had desecrated the Spanish flag by wearing it as a garment and as part of a striptease. So, as I say, I had to go over there to try to straighten matters out, and I tell you, it was no easy matter. It took every moment of my time so that I had no opportunity to get in touch with you. I m deeply sorry, dearest Jane."

"I understand, Manuel darling!" she said, smiling bravely and placing her free hand on his—which, if you remember, was on top of her other one.

"I am glad you do, Jane. I really felt badly about having to cancel our date for New Year's Eve. It is such a special time for people in love. But I do have a bit of a bone to pick with you."

"You mean my date with Percy Byron Browning? I—I'm afraid I went out with him simply to annoy you. He means nothing to me."

"He's very handsome."

"Not as handsome as you, Manuel darling."

"Why thank you, Jane!"

"It's true, Manuel, but unlike Percy Byron Browning, good looks are not all there is to you. He is all surface."

"I rather *thought* you might have dated him to annoy me, and you certainly did. But, I confess, I probably deserved to be treated so."

"Oh darling!" she cried, and would have placed a hand on his but they were both already on or under his. "We've both behaved rather childishly."

"Indeed we have."

"Well," she smiled, "let's put it all behind us now, darling. And to show you that all is well, I'll buy you a cup of coffee. After all this, I think we both need one."

"That is most gracious of you, Jane. Uh—do you mind if I smoke?"

"Of course not, darling! I know it's not politically correct, but I just adore a man who smokes a pipe!"

Manuel felt in his pocket and a frown came over his handsome brow.

"You know, I think I left my pipe in the car. Do you mind if I go out and get it? The Lamborghini is in the parkade just across the way from the Auditorium Annex, so I won't be long."

"Of course I don't mind, darling! I'll wait till you come back to get the coffee so it won't get cold."

Manuel had been gone for but a few minutes when a brazen, flaunting, obtrusive voice split the welkin—or it would have had it sounded outdoors.

(It was later discovered that cracks had appeared in the ceiling of the cafeteria.)

"Well, well!" said the voice sarcastically. "If it isn't lovely young Jane Doe from the free, open, clean and innocent Canadian Prairies!"

Jane looked up to stare into the face, as you've probably surmised, of Yvette la Flambee. This, Jane sensed, would be the moment of truth either for herself or for Yvette la Flambee. Would she prove a valiant, formidable and victorious matador—matadoress—matadora? She seemed to remember reading that there had been a few women who had gone into the ring with the bull, but the metaphor broke down—as all metaphors do if pressed too far—for la Flambee was the Panther, not the bull—hardly the bull.

"Actually," taunted la Flambee, her visible green eye blazing at Jane, "I think your Prairies are rather boring—dull—flat—bleak."

"That's because you don't know them."

"I know them plenty well enough—as much as I ever want to, thank you very much."

"That is your misfortune, not mine" said the new self-possessed Jane Doe.

"I don't suppose you'll be at Janine's party on Friday night?" demanded La Flambee, hands on hips, lower jaw jutting out like Mussolini's.

"I had not heard she was having one, and as far as that goes, I'm not all that fond of parties."

"No, I suppose you are not!" said Yvette caustically.

"Now what is that supposed to mean?" said the new, assertive Jane Doe, not seeking to be combative but prepared to be if the situation were to demand that she should be.

"It means," sneered Yvette, glaring at Jane with her visible green, snake-like eye, "that a mere Barbie doll like you cannot keep Manuel Fernando de Ortega y Diaz de Rodriguez away from me, Yvette la Flambee. They don't call me the Panther for nothing, for the Panther I am, and I exult in the title, because what the Panther wants, the Panther seizes!"

"Well we'll just have to see about that!" said Jane, rising to the challenge—and to her feet—and yes, in her five-inch stilettos she did tower over Yvette. "Panthers have been hunted down and killed, you know!"

"I'd like to see you do that to me!"

"I warned you before, you're dealing with the new Jane Doe!"

"Humph!"

"Furthermore," Jane asserted triumphantly, "Barbie doll or not, I am the woman Manuel loves!"

"Oh? And what would you say if I told you I had been in his bed!"

After the initial shock of this bombshell which briefly brought back her old fears, Jane recovered her composure and her faith in Manuel—and her new self-confidence.

"I'd say it was a lie, but I wouldn't put it past you to have tried, you little slut!"

"Slut! Who are you calling a slut!"

"I'm calling you a slut, Yvette la Flambée!"

"I'll scratch your eyes out, Bimbo!"

And with that the Panther bared her claws and lunged at Jane. Tall and formidable in her twelve point seven centimetre heels, Jane, with great finesse warded off the Panther's attack and with the flat of her hand registered a resounding blow across la Flambee's cheek.

"Ow!" shrieked the Panther. "I'll kill you for that!"

Again the Panther sprang, and all over Yum-Yum's cafeteria patrons and staff dove for cover as Jane met la Flambee's assault with a blow to the shoulder that sent her reeling back against the table behind her.

"Oh, so you want to play rough!" shrieked the Panther renewing her attack by lunging at Jane and grabbing her by the hair. "I'll pull out those long, voluptuous, golden tresses by the roots!"

"Ow!" cried Jane, for Yvette had tugged so hard at her hair that she felt perhaps the Panther had pulled her long, golden, voluptuous tresses out by the roots. But the valor of the new Jane Doe was not to be dissuaded by mere pain.

"Two can play that game!" she cried as she rallied to the counter-attack and in her turn grabbed the glossy, black locks of Yvette la Flambee and pulled hard at them. To her shock and surprise, with a loud tearing sound followed by a wild scream from the Panther, Yvette's whole scalp came off in Jane's hands.

"Oh good heavens!" exclaimed Jane.

Yvette released her grasp on Jane's hair and fell back, and Jane, in wide-eyed amazement looked on her adversary, no longer the glamorous, seductive femme fatale of the raven-black locks, but a pitiful, sniveling, mousy creature with the shortest, skimpiest, dun-colored hair she had ever seen.

"Oh!" shrieked Yvette, clutching her head. "A-a-ah!"

Whereupon she turned on her five-inch stiletto heel and fled toward the exit.

The patrons and staff, perceiving that calm had returned looked up to see *Janea triumphans* holding in her hand, not the head of Holofernes but Yvette la Flambee's black wig, for indeed that was what Jane had pulled from her adversary's head.

"I bet your boobs are phony too!" cried the victorious new Jane Doe after the defeated and retreating erstwhile Panther.

"Oh my goodness!" exclaimed the old Jane Doe. "Did I say boobs?"

Just as Yvette reached the door to make her hurried exit from the cafeteria she met Manuel returning from his expedition to retrieve his pipe.

"A-a-ah!!" she screamed in horror and distress and flung herself past him and raced up the stairs to ground level as fast as her twelve-point-seven-centimetre shod feet could carry her and fled the scene stage right as though pursued by a bear.

"Who was that who just ran out like stricken deer?" asked Manuel on rejoining Jane.

"More like a stricken panther," said Jane.

"What! Yvette la Flambee?"

"Most of her," said Jane, holding up the wig and giving a quick account of what had happened.

"Well I'll be—! But then, I think she also has a glass eye. That's why she always combed her hair—her wig—over the left one."

"Oh!" exclaimed Jane, now moved to pity for her former rival and adversary. "The poor soul!"

"Yes," said Manuel. "Perhaps it explains a lot."

"But—but how do you know that, Manuel . . . ?" asked Jane, a little tremulously, for surely—surely Yvette had not, as she had said, been in Manuel's bed.

"Ah, nothing to trouble you, Jane my dearest," said Manuel, seeming to sense her fears. "You see, I invited a few friends up to my penthouse during the holidays before I was suddenly called away to Spain. La Flambee was not one of them, but somehow she heard about it and arrived at the same time as some of my invited guests into whose company she had managed to ingratiate herself."

"Wearing nothing under her sable coat?" exclaimed Jane apprehensively.

"Wha—? No, though one might have expected as much. Actually she was wearing a cat suit."

"Most appropriate for the Panther—and very seductive."

"Yes, on both counts. However, she had already consumed a large quantity of alcohol before she arrived, and since she seems to have no restraint whatever in the matter of spirits and, I suspect, a low tolerance, she passed out after her first drink at my party. There was nothing to do but lay her out on my bed."

"Oh!" cried Jane, greatly relieved. "So that's what she meant when she said she had been in your bed. She had been *on* it. Of course," she added hurriedly, "I didn't believe for a second that she'd been in it!"

"I should certainly hope not, Jane. But in her stupor, Yvette was muttering all sorts of things which sounded very strange, but we could make neither head nor tail of them until everyone got up to leave, and we struggled to revive her. Her hair—her wig—fell away from the eye she keeps carefully hidden, and we all thought it looked decidedly artificial. Also, in all her contortions as we tried to bring her around, she swearing all the time like a trooper in German—"

"In German!"

"*Jahwohl*! Anyway, in her efforts to resist our getting her to her feet, she knocked her hand bag to the floor and it burst open and spilled out all its contents, among which, besides the mask to go with her cat suit—why on earth she brought that?—"

"I can well imagine!" exclaimed Jane, envisaging a masked, naked Yvette stretched out seductively and enticingly on Manuel's bed.

"Wha—? Oh—yes—I think I know what you're thinking. But as I was saying, there was also a photograph, dated Dusseldorf 1942, of a man in the uniform of the Waffen SS and identified with a number as Fahnrich Helmut Schlamp, and written underneath was '*Dein Grossvater*.' Yvette la Flambee may be her legal name, but I feel almost certain it was not the one with which she began her life. Of course, she is not to blame for the actions of her grandfather, but no doubt his involvement with the Nazis is not something she cares to have known. So Yvette is almost certainly not French. The wig is not the only thing false about her."

"My goodness!" exclaimed Jane. "What a bizarre tale! I suppose one ought to feel sorry for the poor woman—probably she's trying to compensate for an unhappy past—but I'm still glad to be rid of her, as I'm sure we will be."

"Yes, I'm sure we will, and I too am glad. But there are more positive ways to compensate for misfortune than those she has adopted. However, I guess one must not judge another too harshly until one has walked a mile in her shoes."

"'There but for the grace of God go I'. But I can't help thinking how funny you'd look," said Jane with an amused smile in spite of the seriousness of the forgoing conversation, "trying to walk a mile in Yvette's five-inch spikes. And," she said, her tone again becoming serious, "I can't help wondering how poor Yvette lost her eye."

"Probably," he said, with a wink and a smirk, "in a fight with an earlier rival."

"Oh—I—She started it!" Jane protested vigorously. "I was only trying to defend myself! But—but," she said, "we never did have our coffee, so let me get it now."

"Actually, Jane, I think it's almost closing time. So perhaps after such trying afternoon, I could take you for dinner?"

"I'd love that, darling," Jane responded eagerly. "But first I must rearrange my golden locks. I'm afraid Yvette left my long voluptuous tresses in rather a mess."

When she had combed out her hair, Jane took Manuel's proferred arm and they left the cafeteria and walked away arm in arm into the setting sun—that is, to the parkade where Manuel had left his car behind which the sun was setting.

CHAPTER THE TWELFTH AND LAST

Manuel and Jane returned Yvette's wig to her by parcel post, and through the exemplary endeavors of CUPW, it arrived in just under two weeks. Manuel and Jane had not attended Janine's party—a wild, rough, rowdy, raucous affair broken up by the police after numerous complaints by the neighbors—at which Yvette, to everyone's surprise, so April, May, June, Julia, Augusta and Catherine told Jane afterwards—had turned up as a redhead and, even more to everyone's surprise, she had remained strangely subdued the whole evening.

Manuel and Jane had, instead, gone dining and dancing, Jane looking particularly ravishing in her blue evening gown and the gold earrings, bracelet and necklace Manuel had brought back for her from Madrid, and Manuel immaculately resplendent in white tie and tails. Afterward they returned to Manuel's penthouse, Jane tingling with excitement and anticipation, for she felt certain Manuel had something very special in mind. Was this the night he would—? The night they would—? Would this be the night of a thousand and one nights rolled into one?

Jane knew now that she was not the woman she had been when she arrived the previous autumn—how long ago it now seemed and yet, in other ways, it seemed but yesterday, so much had happened—in exciting, worldly, decadent, wicked but gorgeously situated Vancouver. Manuel had had a profound effect on her. She had become less diffident and less inhibited—though she hoped she had not become too uninhibited—less fearful, more confident, more aware of who and what she was and of what she wanted. But she realized, too, that she had had an effect on Manuel, as he himself had often told her. The arrogance had vanished and, though he remained very aristocratic, he was a gentler, kinder, more considerate aristocrat, the truly noble nobleman that an aristocrat is supposed to be. It was hard to believe that she, Jane Doe, a simple girl from the free, open, clean and innocent Canadian Prairies could have drawn out these qualities, made him into the new man he had become, but it seemed that indeed she had. Even harder was it to believe that such a girl as she had won the heart of such a distinguished man as Manuel Fernando de Ortega y Diaz de Rodriguez. It was the sort of thing that happened only in Harlequin Romances, yet here she was, the woman this aristocratic Spaniard professed to love, and Jane had to confess that in her royal blue, off-the-shoulder, white-ermine-trimmed evening gown, long white gloves, jewelry of pure gold and gold high heels—now only four inches or ten point one centimetres since she no longer had to put Yvette la Flambee in her place, though she kept her five-inch heels in reserve for emergencies—looked for all the world like a fairy tale princess, or lady of chivalric romance, or, for that matter, the heroine of a mass circulation paperback novel.

As soon as they entered the living room of his penthouse—where only a single pale blue light glowed in a lamp on an end table in a far corner—Manuel took her into his arms.

"Oh Jane! My Jane!" he said, almost crushing her in his strong, passionate, masculine embrace. "Oh Jane! I love you so! I want you!"

"Oh Manuel!" she cried throwing her smooth, slender, shapely elegantly gloved arms about his neck. "My Manuel! I'm yours Manuel! Take me, Manuel! Oh, take me!"

"You mean—?"

"Yes, Manuel darling, I do mean—"

"Oh, but Jane, my dearest, I'm not sure we're in that kind of novel!"

"Oh," said Jane, disappointment audible in her voice. "Maybe you're right." But the suddenly she cried, "Manuel! I've just remembered something that makes me feel sure we *are* in that kind of novel!"

"Oh! What is that, Jane? Tell me! Oh, please tell me!"

"Remember back in CHAPTER TWO—the day that it rained and you drove me downtown?—that you said there was another woman inside me trying to get out? Surely that was foreshadowing, for I'm sure that woman has been striving to come out ever since I met you, and now she is out. Otherwise why would I let my hair fall to my shoulders in long, voluptuous tresses but that you said I would look so well if I did? Why would I buy, almost against my will, a pair of red four inch, or ten point one centimetre, high heels and wear my skirts shorter than I've ever worn before except for the reason that you said they would show off my lovely, shapely legs to better advantage?"

"Yes—yes! You may be right! But I thought you always said you did those things to please yourself."

"Well, yes, but if you had not suggested—But does it matter, Manuel?"

"No, not to me it doesn't."

"Good, because there's something else."

"Something else, Jane?" cried Manuel eagerly.

"Yes! That very night I had a dream. I was at a ball—I'll leave out some of the irrelevant details since our readers know what they are anyway and we don't want to bore them with repetition—but at the end of the dream you and I were dancing, and I was—I was completely—I was altogether—I was utterly—I was stark naked!" she blurted out finally.

"Stark n—n—na—completely n—nu—totally unc—uncl—uncla—altogether in the altogether!" he stammered.

"I had nothing on but my new red high heels, and I was totally unperturbed, completely at ease and relaxed. Now if that isn't foreshadowing, I don't know what is!"

"Oh yes, Jane, I'm sure it is!" asserted Manuel, "If it is not, then I am not the literary critic—well, a PhD student on the way to becoming a literary critic—that I think I am. But Jane, I am also a *gentilhombre Espanol*, a man of honor. Rather than violate a maiden's chaste treasure by taking advantage of her innocence and eagerness, I am pledged by birth, upbringing and tradition to defend her honor to the death."

"Oh, I know that, Manuel, and I admire it in you, but if you are worried about your honor, remember that in *A Mixture of Frailties* Davidson Roberts—"

"That's Robertson Davies," corrected Manuel.

"Robertson Davies to be sure," said Jane, "but what he says through a couple of his characters is that chastity is having the body in the soul's keeping."

"Yes, true, *vrai, verdadero*. Very true. Still, I would feel better if first of all, I—"

Just at that minute, the telephone rang, and since Manuel had given his valet Miguel and his chef Francisco the night off—the reader may be inclined to speculate as to Manuel's motives for doing so as also for leaving on only a single blue light, but because this novel is written from the third person limited omniscient point of view, and that point of view is Jane's, we are not permitted to know Manuel's motives—and because he was standing right beside the instrument, after first grumbling "Darn!" he answered it.

"Manuel Fernando de Ortega y Diaz de Rodriguez speaking," he said in English—the last word at least was in English—but immediately he switched to Spanish. "*Si—Tio Pedro?—Muerte!*"

Jane stepped back from him, stunned by the implications of what she was hearing, for though she spoke no Spanish, from Manuel's conversations she knew "*Tio*" was "uncle" and *muerte*, obviously derived from the Latin *mors, mortis*, Spanish being a Romance language, surely must mean "dead." Thus she gathered that Manuel's uncle had died.

Then, her hand went to her mouth as she was stunned by a sudden revelation. Manuel's uncle dead! That meant that Manuel was now Don Manuel, *el Duque de Pontevedra y Alicante*. But if so, as surely it must be, what was to become of poor, simple Jane Doe from the free, open, clean and innocent Canadian Prairies? Could *el Duque de Pontevedra y Alicante* marry such an ordinary girl socially so far beneath him? She feared not, and her heart sank.

Suddenly Manuel drew himself to attention.

—Oh! thought Jane. How handsome he looks, how splendid! Oh! Oh! And to think he was almost mine!

"*Su Majestad*!" said Manuel into the receiver.

—"*Su Majestad*!" The King of Spain! The King speaking personally to Manuel! Manuel was speaking personally to the King of Spain! Might Lloyd George also have known his father, his father known Lloyd George?

Manuel, in fact, spoke very little, but listened attentively to his sovereign, saying only at respectful intervals, "*Si, mio Soberania*." Then finally, with a formal bow, he said, "*Gracias, mio Soberania*," and replaced the receiver. For some moments, as as he stood staring in silent amazement at the wall he seemed almost unaware of the presence of Jane staring at him apprehensively.

"M—Manuel?" ventured Jane, striving to hold back the tears that welled up in her lovely and soulful azure eyes.

"Jane!" he exclaimed turning to her. "The most amazing news! My Uncle Pedro Federico de Ortega y Diaz de Rodriguez de Sanchez y Martinez y Navasquez is dead—uh—the details are rather sordid—heart attack while making love to his flamenco dancer mistress who seems to have disappeared—but that means that—"

"That you are now *el Duque de Pontevedra y Alicante*," sobbed Jane unable to hold back the river of tears that now came flooding down her cheeks, "and a poor, humble member of the Third Estate, a mere commoner like Jane Margaret Doe from the free, open clean and innocent Canadian Prairies cannot possibly have any place in your life!"

"Jane! Jane!" he said, taking her by the shoulders and drawing her to him. "What are you saying? What do you mean there's no place for you in my life? How can you possibly think that?" He gently lifted her chin and with the most kindly and loving of smiles looked straight into her tear-filled eyes. "Dry your tears, dearest Jane! Of course, there will be a place for you in my life!"

"Oh, how can that be, Manuel—*Don Manuel*—your Grace?"

"By becoming her Grace *Dona Juana Marguerita de Doe y Ortega y Diaz de Rodriguez, Duquesa de Pontevedra y Alicante*!"

"M—Manuel—?"

"Jane, I want you to be my wife, my duchess, *mia duquesa*."

"Your—your duchess?"

"Yes, Jane, my darling. What else would I want you to be?"

"But—but—"

"There are no buts, Jane. Here," he said dropping to one knee in front of her. "Jane, I wish you do me the great honor of becoming the Duchess of Pontevedra y Alicante."

"Me, Manuel? Me, Jane Doe, a mere—"

"Oh, for heaven's sake, Jane! Mere my thumb! Did you not tell me you were related to the Duke of Argyle? But I would not care a fig if you were not. Were I King Cophetua and you a beggar maid, I would marry you, or were I the Czar of Russia—if they still had czars—or even the Akound of Swat, and you but a lowly peasant girl, I would still marry you. But since you are sprung from aristocracy, it is only proper that you should now return to your roots. Besides, descent from a duke will give you an easy introduction into the Spanish aristocracy, though your beauty and charm will readily overcome their reserve. I can think of no one more fit, no one finer, better to be the Duchess of Pontevedra and Alicante!"

"Oh Manuel!" she cried dropping to her knees and throwing her arms about his neck. "Oh, Manuel!"

"Then," he said standing up and drawing her after him, "arise *Dona Juana Marguerita*, as you soon will be."

"Oh, Manuel, to you, darling, I will always remain just plain Jane!"

"Hardly plain, Jane, but yes, you were Jane when I fell in love with you, and in my heart Jane you shall always be."

"And it was as Manuel that I fell in love with you, not with *el Duque de Pontevedra y Alicante*—though, of course, I do love the Duke of Pontevedra and Alicante for he is you and you are *ipse* and *ipse* is he!"

"Oh Jane!" he exclaimed. "My Jane!" And he planted a long, lingering, warm, passionate, affectionate, loving and very nice kiss on her soft, warm eager lips. "But to get back to where we were before the phone rang, I was about to—Well, wait here just a minute. It's easier if I show you."

He turned and rushed into the bedroom from which in hardly more than moments he returned carrying a minute, velvet-covered box in the palm of his hand, dropped once again to his knees before her, opened the box, took her left hand in his and slid onto the fourth finger the most magnificent, the most splendid diamond solitaire Jane had ever seen.

"Oh Manuel! It's beautiful! But you shouldn't—"

"I didn't. It was my grandmother's, but now it's yours, for *Abuela* gave it to me before I left Spain for Canada, telling me I must give it to the woman she had seen in the cards."

"Oh Manuel! I am honored to wear it! It's—it's magnificent! I never dreamed I'd ever wear on my finger such a splendid ring as this! There are just no words to express how I feel!"

"And dearest Jane," he said, rising to his feet and taking her into his arms, "there are just no words to express the joy I feel that you have consented to be my wife! Uh—you did consent, didn't you?"

"Oh Manuel! Of course I did! Not in so many words, but surely you cannot doubt that—Do you want it in so many words?"

"Only for the joy of hearing you say them, dearest Jane."

"Oh Manuel! Of course I'll be—Actually, I'm not sure if you ever really asked me."

"Surely you cannot doubt—Do you want me to ask you?"

"Only for the joy of hearing you do so, darling."

"Jane, my beloved, will you marry me?"

"Yes."

"Well, I'm glad we've got that settled. So now—?"

"Now? well, I've never done this before, but I think the lady begins by peeling off her gloves and unfastening the gentleman's tie."

"Yes, and then I think the gentleman unfastens the back of the lady's dress."

"Yes, and then the lady undoes the buttons on the gentleman's shirt."

"While he gently strokes her back."

"O-o-oh! That feels so lovely, Manuel!"

"Oh, I'm glad you like it. Your skin is so lovely and smooth! Then I think the gentleman pushes the upper part of the lady's dress away from her—Jane! You're not wearing a bra!"

"Oh—I wasn't trying to be—It's just that I don't have a strapless one to go with this gown. I spent all my budget and the money my parents sent me on shoes and mini-skirts—Then," she resumed her previous cataloguing of what a lady should do in these circumstances, "I think it's the lady's turn to pull his shirt tails away from his trousers, open the front of his shirt and lay her cheek against his chest."

"While he pushes her gown down past her hips and—O-o-oh! That feels so lovely, Jane!"

"And your chest is so rugged, Manuel! But then I think the lady steps out of her dress."

"And then the gentleman lifts the lady into his arms."

"And then the lady kicks off her shoes and peels off her nylons so that she is now completely naked!" said Jane, happy at last to be able to utter that word without embarrassment.

"And then the gentleman carries her into his bedroom."

"And then—"

And then Manuel closed the door.

Reader, they made love, for who can say them nay? But you are not permitted to see them together in that sublime moment of happy intimacy, nor will you be given another glimpse of lovely young Jane Doe with nothing on but her engagement ring, for Manuel was right: this is not that kind of a novel. Over Manuel and Jane on their night of love hover the silent, gentle, benevolent wings of blissful peace and joy and that happiness promised by our everliving novelist in setting forth.

* * * *

The following morning, Francisco, returning from his night off, found Jane in Manuel's second-best robe and her high heels—Manuel's slippers being much too large for her exquisite and elegant feet, and besides, high heels are more glamorous—preparing breakfast.

"*Senorita* Hane!" he protested indignantly. "I must demand to know why it is that you have invaded my keetchen to prepare ze breakfast for the *Senor* Ortega y Diaz de Rodriguez in ze patron's second best robe and your high heels!"

"*Buenos Diaz*, Francisco," said Jane, turning to smile benignly on him. "Yes, I know it is wrong of me to take over your kitchen, but I beg your forgiveness and your indulgence just this once, for a Canadian bride should prepare breakfast for her man at least once, for I will have few, if any, opportunities when I am your master's wife."

"*Su esposa! Su mujer!* Hees wife!"

"Yes, Francisco, your master has asked me to marry him."

"*Carramba!*"

"*Carramba*! indeed, Francisco. So you see, this is a very special morning for me, and I hope that, in the unusual circumstances, you will forgive me."

"Eet ees eeregular, but perhaps on thees occasion—"

Just at that moment, Manuel, wearing his third-best robe and carrying his first-best one over his arm, emerged from the bedroom.

"Jane! What is the future *Duquesa de Pontevedra y Alicante* doing, soiling her dainty hands slaving like a scullery maid in the kitchen in her high heels and my second-best robe?"

"I hardly seemed right to wear your best one, darling, and as for slaving—"

But here Francisco interrupted, unable to contain his surprise.

"Ze future *Duquesa de Pontevedra y Alicante*!"

"Yes, Francisco," said Jane. "Believe it or not, last evening none other than his Majesty the King of Spain phoned to confer the title on your master. He is now **Don** *Manuel de Ortega y Diaz de Rodriguez*, and he has asked me to be his wife—his duchess."

Francisco fell to his knees to kiss Jane's hand.

"*Mia Duquesa!*"

"Well, I'm not the duchess yet, Francisco. It is to your master that you should kneel."

"*Oh si! Perdona Don Manuel! Perdona!*"

"Oh, get up off your knees Francisco and stop kissing my foot!" exclaimed Manuel. "I don't expect my employees to grovel! But, yes, *Senorita* Jane soon will be a duchess—as soon as the university term is over and we can fly over to Spain to be married—so your homage is not misplaced. But," asked Manuel, "I still want to know, Jane, why you are—"

"Why the future Duchess of Pontevedra y Alicante is soiling her dainty hands slaving in your kitchen to prepare breakfast for the Duke, her future husband? Because it's an old Canadian custom that a new bride should do that, for when I am in fact the Duchess of Pontevedra y Alicante, I doubt if I'll ever be given the chance."

"Oh—well—" said Manuel, his anger abating, "if it's an old established custom—you know how much I respect that sort of thing."

"Yes, I do know that darling. That is why I have made so bold. But now, you go and sit in your favorite arm chair and read this morning's *Globe and Mail*, and I will have your breakfast ready in a jiffy."

"A jiffy?" queried Manuel.

"*Si*," queried Francisco. "A heefy?"

"A very short time. It's a colloquialism."

"Ah!"

Later, over coffee, Jane at Manuel's insistence now wearing his best robe while he, at Jane's insistence, wore his second-best one, Manuel said, "Jane! That was a most delicious breakfast!" Then assuring himself that Francisco was out of earshot, he added, "The best I've ever been served! You are a splendid cook, my darling—a quality not normally found in duchesses."

"Well, after all, darling, I always expected to have to cook, for I was not raised to be a duchess. Never in my wildest dreams did I ever expect to be a duchess, and I still haven't got used to the idea that I will be one. I hope I will be worthy of the honor."

"You will make a splendid duchess, Jane! You were born to be a duchess, a princess, a queen, an empress—but a duchess is the best that I can offer. You have all the requisite qualities—beauty—" He paused, lost for a moment in thought, casting his eyes toward the ceiling. "Actually, most of the duchesses I've known have been rather plain, or as Dylan Thomas said, horse-faced. Actually, I think he said horses are duchesses-faced. But a duchess *ought* to be beautiful, and I'm so very glad you are. Now let's see, what else? Intelligence—" Again he stared up at the ceiling. "Actually, most duchesses, are rather dim-witted, come to think of it—but again, I am glad that you are so intelligent. A duchess *should* be intelligent. Now, what else? Poise—Actually, most duchesses I know are rather stuffy and snooty, rather than poised. Well again, a duchess *ought* to have poise. Grace—well, most duchesses are more condescending than gracious. Good manners—but for that matter, most duchesses are boors. Well, you have all the qualities a duchess ought to have.

"Oh Manuel! You flatter me. But there is something about which I wonder—now that we are to be a duke and a duchess, what about our degrees? I've had my heart set for a long time on obtaining my PhD."

"And why should you not obtain it? I want you to obtain it. Living in Canada has had a beneficial effect on me, Jane dearest," he said with a warm, loving and slightly whimsical smile. "I've absorbed some of the ideas of ideas of the Women's Movement. No doubt ther will always be something of the arrogant Castillian about me . . ."

"What's bred in the bone . . . ?" queried Jane.

"Indeed."

"As Robertson Davies says!" they both exclaimed together.

"Well," said Jane, also whimsically, "as the future Duchess of Pontevedra y Alicante, I'll make sure you don't become too arrogant."

"I hope you will, Jane. You're wonderful."

"And you're wonderful too, Manuel. I'm glad I eventually realized it. I'm glad you persisted in making me get to know you."

"I'm glad I did too. But to return ot our former topic, I still want to get my PhD too. As *Duque de Pontevedra y Alicante* I am *ex officio* Chancellor of the University of Cordoba. (I find it hard to see *Tio* Pedro in that role.) So I want at least to be the academic equal, so to speak, of those under me. Of course, Jane, you are guaranteed a professorship—if you want it. But I do not have to spend all my time in Spain; so I will not object if you prefer to seek a position elsewhere. There! You see, I have been influenced by the Woman's Movement."

Jane threw her arms about him and kissed him.

"Oh Manuel darling, you sexist reactionary! I love you! You're really wonderful!"

"Not nearly so wonderful as you, my darling Jane, you wild-eyed, misguided radical!"

And so, Reader, she married him.

At the end of the summer, after she and Manuel had completed Professor Culver Hoople's summer course in Dickens—in which they both earned *As*—wearing a gorgeous gown of white silk satin adorned with pearls and with a long train born by a bevy of Manuel's young nieces, with Manuel's Sister Sophia as bride's maid and his cousin who lives in Caregena's wife as matron of honor—both of whom became Jane's fast friends—and with April, May, June, Julia, Augusta and Catherine—flown over at Manuel's expense—as honorary bride's maids, in the chapel of the British Embassy in Madrid, the Bishop of the Spanish Reformed Episcopal Church presiding, assisted by the Reverend Canon William Rowan and Jane's rector from Saskatoon—both also flown over at Manuel's expense, and in the presence of Their Hispanic Majesties the King and Queen of Spain, with Jane's parents—also flow over at Manuel's expense (as the largest land owner in Spain Manuel was exceedingly wealthy)—aglow with happiness and pride, Jane Margaret Doe from the flat, empty, wild, wind-swept Canadian Prairies* became *Dona Juana Marguerita de Doe y Ortega y Diaz de Rodriquez, La Duquesa de Pontevedra y Alicante.* The Duke and Duchess spent their honeymoon cruising the Mediterranean aboard the Duke's yacht, stopping at many an exotic port-of-call where splendor falls on castle walls and lofty summits old in story, where long lights shake across the lakes and wild cataracts leap in glory.

Donald, already fallen into degeneracy and dissipation on cheap booze and glue sniffing, on hearing of Jane's engagement and impending marriage, fell into total degeneracy and was last seen trying to sell pencils, cheap balloons and other gew-gaws at the corner of Roson Avenue and and Granville Street.**

Handsome Percy Byron Browning, the other hopeful for Jane's hand, on completing his PhD, found himself unable to choose among his bevy of adoring undergraduate admirers, and so, at his father's expense, he shipped himself off on a South Sea Islands Cruise during which he was hired on as a professor at the University of Vanuatu where he soon found himself surrounded by a bevy of bare-breasted undergraduate admirers, a circumstance which seemed at first to compound his difficulties, but as he became accustomed to the relaxed, easy-going life style and mores of those southern climes, he decided there was nothing to be gained by being miserable and unhappy in paradise.

Yvette la Flambee—or whoever she really was—completed her PhD in a whirlwind of effort of which few believed her capable and returned to Moscow where she sought out Colonel of Militia Sergei Alexeivich

---

* Thought I was going to say something else didn't you? Gotcha!

** Learning of his condition after their return from their honeymoon, the Duke and Duchess of Pontevedra y Alicante, out of pity, had a social agency seek him out and then paid for his rehabilitation. On completing his rehabilitation, Donald joined the French Foreign Legion. (Ed.)

Timoshenko and, by fair means or foul, for she certainly had an extensive repertoire of both, persuaded him to marry her—her black wig now having associations she preferred to forget, remained a red head, explaining to Sergei that she had really always been one but that the People's Commissar for Furs had demanded she be a brunette for the modeling tour—and moved with him to Ulaan Bataar in the Mongolian Republic where Sergei Alexeivich had been appointed military attache to the Russian Embassy and where she obtained an Assistant Professorship in English at Genghis Khan Memorial University, an equal opportunity employer.

April, May, June, Julia, Augusta and Catherine each found young men—or the young men found them, there remains some uncertainty—in the Departments of Comparative Literature, Philosophy, Linguistics, Creative Writing, French, and Computer Science.

Alison, the Reading Room attendant—with whom Jane had become reconciled after the former's nearly disastrous faux pas—turned down the marriage proposal of an oil-rich sheik from the United Arab Emirates, for she had no wish to be one wife in four—and who knows how many concubines—but was most gratified by the attentions of Jean-Gascon de Rochefoucault, *Duc de Orleans et Blois,* a friend of Manuel Fernando de Ortega y Diaz de Rodriguez, *Duque de Pontevedra y Alicante.* Continuing her studies toward her PhD, she sponsored a literary competition to write a novel about a lovely young graduate student from Saskatchewan at the University of British Columbia who met and won the heart of a handsome, enormously wealthy Spanish aristocrat fellow graduate student, which Ron Harriott, reappearing in these pages again after successfully completing the treatment program for drug and alcohol abuse, and writing, for some reason, under a female *nom de plume,* won with his submission.

The English Department of the University of British Columbia continues to confer MAs and PhDs on capable and worthy candidates and occasionally, since mistakes will happen, on academic frauds like the editor of this novel.

Yum-Yum's Cafeteria continues to dispense its excellent coffee.

And oh yes, Jane and Manuel lived happily ever after.

What else did you expect in a novel like this?